245 Pages

Complete

THE LAZARUS LONGMAN CHRONICLES

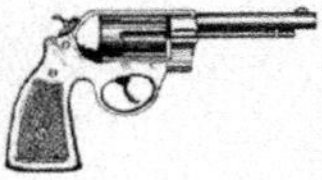

ONE DIME

ONYX CITY

P. J. Thorndyke

LONDON

Number 3

1888

Onyx City
By P. J. Thorndyke

Contents

Chapter One

In which a journal of some import eludes our hero

The butler who admitted Lazarus Longman to the house on Cavendish Square had the air of one who had nothing of enjoyment left in life but the promise of retirement. He was sizing Lazarus up as if determining whether he should be sent around to the tradesman's entrance, when Lazarus spoke.

"I don't have a card. I have been in correspondence with Mr. Walters and he invited me. The name's Longman."

"Ah, yes, sir," the butler said, a ghost of a smile on his lips. "I have been told to expect you. This way please."

The house must have been a fine one once, but now the floorboards creaked under threadbare carpets and gloom hung about the place like a pall. It looked like it had never been a family home. The only pictures on the walls were mezzotints of bridges and watercolors of foreign parts. Cobwebs dangled from the lamp fittings and chandeliers. If Cornelius Walters employed a maid, Lazarus decided, she should be flung out on her ear.

They entered a library, although for all the foliage about, Lazarus wasn't sure that it didn't double as a conservatory. Skylights and windows let in large amounts of light, which couldn't have been good for the books that were lined up on mahogany shelves, interspersed with pots dangling their green tendrils onto the shelves below. Occasional oddities like mammal skulls and small antiquities gave the place the air of a haphazard museum.

In a wicker chair sat an elderly man with a small pair of spectacles perched on the tip of his nose. His hair was snow white and swept across a balding pate. "Ah, Mr. Longman!" said the man. He did not rise from his chair but motioned to an identical one opposite.

Lazarus sat down and accepted the old man's hand. "Mr. Walters, it is a pleasure to finally meet you."

"Likewise, sir. And I must say that you are younger than I imagined. Tea?"

"Please."

"Bring us a pot, Peterson," Walters said to the butler, who nodded and ducked out of the room.

Lazarus loosened his collar and looked around at all the plants. "Is all this humidity good for the books?"

"Not particularly. But these books you see here are not in the least bit valuable. Junk mostly, but I can never bear to throw a book out. My library upstairs is where I keep my real treasures. The conservatory is merely where I choose to spend most of my time. The bones ache at my age, you see. I only keep books in here because there is no other place for them."

"And it is a particular volume that I am here to examine," said Lazarus.

"I know, and I must apologize for wasting your

time."

"Wasting my time?"

"You see, I did possess the journal you spoke of and fully intended to sell it to you, but alas, a fellow came calling with a better offer and I let him have it. I know it wasn't particularly polite of me, but I am trying to run a business here, such as it is. My fortunes of late have dipped a little, as I am sure you can tell."

"That's quite all right. I am a little disappointed though. And a little surprised that another individual should express an interest in such an obscure curiosity."

"It's not too hard to fathom," said Cornelius. "The journal, though one of a kind, is an invaluable resource on the mountain peoples of Siam. It is a firsthand account and the mysterious fate of its author makes it doubly interesting."

"The author's fate is no mystery," said Lazarus. "Thomas Tyndall died in Siam."

"Under extremely unusual circumstances, as I'm sure you will agree."

"Nevertheless, I find it uncanny that somebody who shares my interest purchased the journal within days of our last correspondence."

"You are very disappointed, I can appreciate that. Allow me to make some way in amends. The gentleman left his calling card, and you may have it should you wish to approach him with an offer." Cornelius rifled through a stack of newspapers and letters on the side table, upon which stood a Japanese bonsai tree in a glass bell jar. He retrieved a calling card and passed it to Lazarus.

It read;

J. C. TURNBULL

Fine Boots, Shoes and Pumps

REPAIRS DONE PROMPTLY

57 Copley Street, Stepney

"A cobbler interested in an explorer's journal of Siam?" asked Lazarus in astonishment.

"A hobby, perhaps. Come to think of it, I don't remember you telling me your profession, Mr. Longman."

"I didn't."

"I suppose it would be crossing the boundaries of professionalism to enquire as to your own interest in the journal?"

"You're right," said Lazarus smartly. "It would." He rose and clutched the rim of his bowler hat. "I must leave you now, I'm afraid. I'm a very busy man."

Just then, Peterson the butler entered, bearing a tea tray.

"Sorry, I can't stop for tea. This was a professional visit after all, and there is little further to discuss. Thank you for your time and the card."

"Not at all, Mr. Longman," said Cornelius Walters. "I wish you all success in your pursuit."

Lazarus gritted his teeth as he stepped out onto the street and heard the door close shut behind him. He was being given the runaround, that much was certain. What was less certain was why.

He spotted the four-wheeler and its horses on the other side of the street. It was a Clarence, known as a 'growler', usually privately owned, although it was becoming more common in recent years to see secondhand examples put into use as Hackney carriages. Often, they showed some trace of the former owner's coat of arms on the side, but this one had a glossy, black finish without a single adornment.

Its door opened and a face was thrust out. Lazarus felt he had seen it before somewhere but could not quite place it.

"With us, Longman," the face said brusquely. Lazarus immediately knew who they were and why there were here; the unadorned carriage, the two men who knew his name and had undoubtedly been waiting for him, following him even. These were men from the bureau.

He felt his feet walking him over to the carriage without remembering giving them the instructions to do so. The last thing he wanted was to get drawn into more entanglements with the government. He felt as if he had only just been released from their clutches, after narrowly avoiding a prison sentence or a swift departure from the world at the hand of a state-employed assassin. In fact, how could he be sure that these men in their carriage weren't just that? But no, why wait two years to kill him?

Two years had passed since he had returned from Egypt in disgrace. Not only had he failed in his mission to return the French Egyptologist Eleanor Rousseau to her fiancé in England, but he had directly disobeyed orders and greatly endangered British relations with the Confederate States of America. The C.S.A.'s ignorance of his involvement in the devastating crash of its dirigible, the *CSS Scorpion II*, was the only thing that had saved Lazarus from being thrown to the wolves. All aboard had been killed but him and Katarina

Mikolavna; the Russian agent whom he had fallen in with.

Or was that fallen in love with?

Two years—and he still thought about her every day. Two years since she had left him gawking on the platform at *Gare Montparnasse* in Paris like a foolish schoolboy. He had accepted that he would never see her again. His brain knew that. But his heart still hadn't received the news.

"Where would you take me?" he asked the men in the carriage.

"To see the Gaffer," said the man who had spoken.

They both wore grey suits. One had a moustache and the other wore spectacles. They had the bored airs of those who rarely left London and spent their lives passing correspondence between others with vastly more exiting lives. Lazarus knew the type.

"I don't suppose either of you know what he wants to see me about?" Lazarus asked. "Or doesn't he tell his lackeys that much?"

Their faces soured and for a moment Lazarus thought he was going to receive a fist in his face. But these two were probably more used to pushing piles of paper around than actual people.

"Just get in, Longman," the man with the spectacles said. "No need to be bloody-minded."

Lazarus did so, and soon they were clattering along Regent Street towards Charing Cross. They headed down Whitehall and turned into an unassuming courtyard beneath a brick arch. There were some other carriages in the yard, their drivers tending to their horses. A casual passerby might have thought the place a mere coach yard. Only a trained military eye would have spotted the camouflaged pillboxes high up on the balconies of the surrounding buildings.

They entered a small tradesman's entrance and climbed a narrow, carpeted stair that led onto a landing with three doors. A portrait of Queen Victoria hung opposite a rectangular window, the light breaking her severe face into a criss-cross of bars.

One of the doors led to a long corridor that extended deep into the unknown depths of whatever building they were now in. Portraits of prime ministers going all the way back to Sir Robert Walpole peered down from the walls. A secret serviceman in a plain dark suit sat by a door with his legs crossed, reading the Times. He looked up at Longman, did not smile, and returned to his paper.

"You know where you are and what to do," said one of Lazarus's escorts.

"Aren't you going to hold my hand when we go in?" Lazarus asked him.

"You're on your own, *treasure hunter*."

The two men departed, leaving Lazarus to open the door and walk in. The secretary rose from her desk and ushered him into the office beyond with a customary knock and opening of the door. She closed it behind him.

Morton sat behind his inordinately large desk and did not rise. Lazarus needed no invitation to occupy the plain chair set before the gargantuan mahogany slab and sat down.

"Good of you to come, Longman," said Morton, rising to pour them both some cognac.

"Had I a choice?"

Morton smiled and handed him his glass. "I've missed you, old fellow."

"I'm afraid the feeling isn't mutual."

"Yes, I understand you've been keeping yourself busy. Lectures at King's College, talks at the British Museum and a book on the Akan people, that sort of thing. Not to mention further pursuits in archaeology and anthropology. Something to do with Siam now, isn't it? Going back to your roots?"

"It's perhaps time that I did."

"Well it's all very commendable. Can't pay all that well though, I'd imagine."

"I do all right."

"And your father? Is he still living in that house in Edmonton?"

"Guardian," Lazarus corrected him. "Yes he is."

"Ill, I heard."

"Pneumonia."

"Second time?"

"Third."

"You know there are some very fine doctors at Guy's Hospital."

"You know I have not the means. Are you suggesting that I work for you again? Is that why I'm here?"

"You're needed. All of our agents are. Difficult days are ahead."

"Except I'm not an agent anymore. You damn near had me thrown in prison after my last assignment."

"And with good reason. Your blatant disregard for orders nearly caused an international crisis."

"Good job everybody onboard that dirigible perished, eh?"

"The truth of the matter is that I've got far too many agents in the field right now and not enough on home turf, which is where things look set to flare up in the foreseeable future."

"What's the business?"

"You have no doubt heard of Otto von Bismarck's visit in two months time."

"The Prussian President? Or is he the Chancellor of the German Empire now? I haven't kept up with the situation."

"Both in effect; they have been merged. Since his League of the Three Emperors fell apart, he has been looking for allies against Russian expansion. His visit to London in November is part of a ploy to side with us and absolutely nothing must interfere with it. Relations with Germany have been strained of late, and although Bismarck is concerned with peace above all else, his new Kaiser is an aggressive sod and will think nothing of declaring war on us regardless of what his chancellor thinks. He's already begun construction on a new navy, and even has colonial desires—which is something new for Germany. The feeling in parliament is that Bismarck must receive British support if only to hold Kaiser Wilhelm by the collar.

"We're worried that some sort of trouble during the visit might stir things up between us and the Germans. Bismarck has made himself thoroughly unpopular with leftists all around the world due to his anti-socialist policies. And we have more than our share of reds here in London. You recall that dreadful business last year?"

"The Trafalgar Square riots? Yes, I was due to give a speech at the British Museum but it had to be called off."

"The East End in particular is a tinderbox awaiting a spark. Revolutionist groups, anarchists, labor strikes. The PM is worried that some of these lunatics might try and assassinate Bismarck. We've got our fair share of Polish Jews too, another group that despise

Bismarck with a passion. None of them can be allowed to get near him."

"I assume you have employed all the requisite security measures."

"Naturally. But we have something else in mind. We need to sink a man deep into the red hot spots in the East End. A sort of spy who can ferry us information on the movements of these groups and let us know if something big is coming down the pipeline."

Lazarus studied his former employer intently. "You can't seriously be suggesting that I might be this man."

"It's perhaps not as exciting as your previous assignments but it's a damn sight less dangerous. Its intelligence gathering. A small job to bring you back into the fold. My trust in you hasn't been completely swept away, Longman, although there are some in my circles who believe you should have been shot as a traitor. I want to prove them wrong. You're a damn good agent and I don't want to lose you. You just need a bit of a chance to prove to us that you're still our man."

"For God's sake, Morton!" Lazarus exclaimed. "I'm an antiquarian! A treasure hunter as your man outside was so quick to call me. I'm not a spy or an undercover policeman. Why on earth do you want me for this thing?"

"For the reasons I have just outlined. And because all my other agents are tied up with more important matters."

"Oh, thank you very much."

"Come off it, I didn't mean it like that. I want you back on my go-to list and you need to show us that you've still got what it takes. Besides, don't you speak Hebrew?"

"I can read Hebrew should the occasion call."

"Can't you apply yourself and see if you can't get an ear for it? It would be of enormous help in infiltrating the Jewish radical clubs."

"Jews in London generally speak Yiddish. Quite different."

"Well, I understand Hebrew is still used in some of their pamphlets and propaganda. Anyway, you wouldn't be working alone. I've arranged for a man to accompany you on your journey into the underworld. Sort of a bodyguard. You'd be the one in charge, there's no mistake about that. I'd like to introduce you tomorrow morning."

"Morton, I still don't think I'm the man. And I'm very busy at the moment."

"Giving lectures and chasing down obscure books? This is national security, man! And this isn't just some plebs beating the war drum. We've reason to believe that the socialists are becoming extremely organized. The Russians may be involved."

Lazarus's heart skipped a beat. For all he knew about Russia, its mention only stirred up one thought in his mind these days. *Katarina.*

"The revolutionist movement is even bigger in Moscow and Saint Petersburg," Morton went on. "And intelligence says that the reds over there have been shipping hardcore rabble-rousers to London to influence and stir things up even more. Something's got to be done or we'll lose control over our own bloody city!"

"And am I to identify these Russians?" Lazarus asked.

"If you have the chance. But you are to report on all developments in socialist circles, Russians, Jews or anybody else."

Russians, thought Lazarus, remembering Katarina's pale breasts and the scent of her perfume, crumpled sheets smelling of their sweat in a Parisian hotel room. Of course it was ludicrous to think that by coming into contact with some of her countrymen he would somehow be drawn closer to her. As the niece of a high-ranking member of the Okhrana, Katarina was no revolutionary. But for some reason, the mention of Russians made the whole business seem not altogether unappealing.

"Who is this fellow I'm to be working with?" he asked.

Chapter Two

In which a fine performance is given at the Lyceum Theatre

By the time Lazarus left Morton's office it was too late to pursue his cobbler in Stepney. That appointment must wait for another day. And besides, he had tickets to the theatre that night and had to go home and get changed. *The Strange Case of Dr. Jekyll and Mr. Hyde* was showing at the Lyceum. The production had opened in Boston the year previously and was currently enjoying great success in London. But Lazarus's interest in the play was more than a mere desire for an evening's entertainment. He had heard of the novella by R. L. Stevenson but had not read it, his academic pursuits leaving little time for the reading of anything but scholarly works. His main reason for choosing this production in particular was that he knew the actor who played both Dr. Jekyll and Mr. Hyde.

He had met Richard Mansfield in New York, shortly after his business in the American Southwest had come to its climax. It was in the wake of Katarina's first departure from his life that he had found himself wandering Broadway, frequenting the saloons and gambling dens of that city of dreamers and philanthropists. He was mustering the courage to return home to London and take up service with the bureau again, postponing the inevitable in a haze of whiskey and opium smoke, when he ran into Mansfield outside of Barnum's American Museum.

A British actor and theater manager with the Union Square Theatre Company, Mansfield was an eccentric, outgoing and endlessly energetic fellow. They had taken to each other immediately and began seeking adventure in New York's shadiest corners; two limeys in a cultural mixing pot that exuded every exotic odor known to man. Lazarus would often attend Mansfield's plays on Broadway and marvel at how the man could perform after a night of girls and liquor. After the shows they would hit the town once more.

Lazarus had rarely had the time to miss old friends in the years that had followed. It was only now in this seeming lull in his life that he began to dwell on past acquaintances and the fun times they had shared. And here was Richard Mansfield himself in London.

The hansom dropped Lazarus off at the pillared entrance to the Lyceum Theatre where a mass of patrons had already gathered. He squeezed past the throng of gentlemen in top hats and overcoats and ladies in their finest evening wear, to the lobby where he was taken to his velvet-lined box seat that overlooked the left of the stage. He rose and smiled politely as the elderly couple with whom he was to be sharing the box sidled in and made themselves comfortable. He looked down on the rows of seats as they gradually filled up. It was to be a full house, confirming the hype the play had elicited from the press and public despite its mixed reviews.

While many journals applauded the play's impressive effects and grotesques, others accused it of relying on spectacle over substance and even claimed

Mansfield was a 'mechanical hack' who, while impressively frightening as the villainous Mr. Hyde, failed to draw much sympathy as the monster's well-meaning alter ego Dr. Jekyll.

Lazarus cared little for reviews. He was here to see his friend and marvel at his much-touted on stage transformation into the walking embodiment of evil that was rumored to have women fainting in the aisles.

Neither the play nor Mansfield's performance disappointed. When he was hunched over, ape-like, as the hideous Mr. Hyde, the audience gasped in horror. It was hard to see that Jekyll and Hyde were played by the same man, as the latter's face was contorted into such a grimace of primal rage, that Lazarus began to doubt the theater company's claims that it was all performance and make up and that no mechanical or illusionary devices were used.

The real shocking part of the play came at the pivotal part of the story, where Mr. Hyde murders an elderly politician by the name of Danvers Carew. Hyde attacked the man brutally with a silver-topped cane, and unleashed such a barrage of blows and stamped on the poor fellow with such ferocity, that several men in the audience leapt out of their seats in alarm, deeming that the violence on stage had surpassed the theatrical.

But when the curtain fell to thunderous applause, the audience rose in a standing ovation. As the bulk of them made their way to the exits, Lazarus descended to the theatre floor and asked around for the manager. He was directed to a thick-set Irishman by the name of Stoker who was modestly accepting the compliments of a pair of theatergoers.

"Excuse me, sir," Lazarus said once the couple had departed. "I am an old friend of Mr. Mansfield. He doesn't know I'm here but I would be most obliged if you could allow me backstage to speak with him."

The man scratched his thick, dark beard. "He's a busy man, sir, being both actor and producer for this play, but I suppose if you're an old friend he won't mind a quick visit. But be mindful, he's usually very tired after a performance."

Lazarus frowned as he was shown backstage. Mansfield had always been buzzing after a performance and ready for a night on the town. The rooms backstage were bustling with activity as stagehands hurried back and forth carrying costumes and props, and actors in various stages of undress chatted and congratulated each other in loud voices.

He eventually found his way to Mansfield's room, but as he approached he heard raised voices coming from within. He held back, not wishing to intrude on anything, but was able to snatch a snippet of the argument. There was a good deal of cursing. Suddenly the door flew open and a tall, thin man with white powder in his hair stormed out, rudely pushing past Lazarus on his way. He recognized him as the fellow who had played Danvers Carew, and caught a faint smear of blood on his lower lip that had begun to dry.

Lazarus knocked on the door and peered in to see Mansfield collapsed in a chair, evidently exhausted, either from the strains of his performance or the recent altercation with his fellow thespian. He turned to look at Lazarus and then leapt up in surprised joy, the worry lines beneath his greasepaint melting away.

"Lazarus, my dear fellow!" he exclaimed, grabbing him by the hand and reaching around to shut the door behind him. "What a welcome surprise this is! Please, take a seat in my humble quarters!" He drew up a battered old chair—a twin to his own—and offered it to Lazarus before flopping back down. He began rummaging around in the cupboard underneath his dressing mirror.

"What the devil was all that about?" Lazarus asked, nodding at the closed door.

"Oh, I fear that I may have overdone my performance tonight," Mansfield replied, producing a half empty bottle of cognac and two glasses. "I do hope that Patrick forgives me. He has warned me of it before, but this night I seemed to have hurt him. My cane struck his lip, although I always try to pull my blows."

"Accidents happen," said Lazarus. "You were really very good. Quite remarkable."

"Thank you, old friend. You don't know how timely your visit is. I am in need of a good companion at the moment."

"Are you all right, Richard?" Lazarus asked. He had noticed Mansfield's hands shaking almost uncontrollably as he drank his cognac quicker than was considered civilized. The man seemed on the verge of some sort of breakdown.

"I fear that I am not well at all, Lazarus. I have been having such frightful nightmares that leave me in the early hours drenched in sweat and gasping for breath."

"You overwork yourself. You always throw yourself into things, and this acting lark is starting to take it out of you."

"It's not just the nightmares. Some days I feel that I am barely in control of myself. Rage grips me at odd times of the day for no apparent reason. I feel as if there is some hideous thing bubbling under my skin, threatening to consume me at any moment. You saw me on stage tonight. I almost lost myself up there and injured poor Patrick."

"Well look at the part you are playing," said Lazarus. "Or should I say 'parts'. You've embarked upon a disturbing character study of this Jekyll and his alter ego, and applied yourself so intensely that it has begun to affect you."

"I am not so sure that I don't have an alter ego of my own."

"How do you mean?"

"Lazarus, you are an old friend and I trust you absolutely. I know that we haven't seen much of each other in recent years, but I hope that time has not eroded the trust between us."

"I can guarantee that it hasn't."

"Then what I am about to tell you must remain between us at all costs. My career, my life even, hangs on your confidence."

"Good God, man, spit it out. There has never been any cause for mistrust between us."

"I must tell you that upon two occasions in recent weeks, I have not woken in my own bed."

"Oh?" said Lazarus with a sly grin. "I don't remember that was ever a cause for concern for you back in New York."

Mansfield did not acknowledge the jest. "I have woken in circumstances most alarming. In an old lime oast downriver, my hands and clothes bloodied."

"A lime oast?"

He nodded. "All alone on the dusty floor of some derelict building without the slightest idea of how I got there."

"Have you ever been there before?"

"No, never! On the first occasion it took me the

best part of the morning to find out where I was and how I was to get home, which I did… eventually. But what has me flummoxed is how and why I wound up there. And whose blood was on my hands."

"It sounds to me that you took a heavy night one evening and got into a fistfight that you don't remember," said Lazarus. "It's happened to both of us before."

Mansfield didn't answer, but reached to pick up a newspaper that had been folded over to display one page in particular. "Have you heard about this?" he said, passing Lazarus the crumpled paper. It was the Evening News dated the eighth of September, which was two days ago.

ANOTHER EAST END MURDER EARLY THIS MORNING IN SPITALFIELDS.

A WOMAN'S THROAT CUT AND HER BODY RIPPED OPEN.

THE LEATHER APRON FOUND.

TERRIBLE DETAILS.

THE ENTRAILS AND THE HEART CUT OUT.

Lazarus had heard of the Whitechapel Murders. Indeed it was hard to avoid the grisly details of what had been happening in the East End in the past month. Three prostitutes had been butchered in the most grotesque manner, all in the slum district of

Whitechapel. The papers were full of it, claiming the killings to be the work of one man and a decided maniac at that.

"Yes, I've read of this," Lazarus murmured, setting the paper aside.

Mansfield regarded him with bloodshot eyes. "Polly Nicols, killed in Buck's Row on August the thirty-first. Annie Chapman, killed in Hanbury Street, September eighth. I awoke in Limehouse directly after these two murders. And I have no memories of those nights. Anything could have happened! I could have done anything..."

"Lord, man!" Lazarus exclaimed. "Surely you are not suggesting..."

"I don't know what I'm suggesting!" he cried. "I'm bloody scared, Lazarus! I don't know what's happening to me!"

"But this is paranoid fantasy! Coincidence and nothing more. And besides, you only mentioned two of the killings. The papers say that there was a third; the earliest. Martha Tabram was also killed in early August. Did you wake in Limehouse then, too?"

"No, I..."

"There, you see? What you are suggesting is simply not credible."

"I don't know what's credible these days. All I know is that something frightful is happening to me that I have absolutely no control over."

"You need rest and perhaps a little diversion," Lazarus said. "How about you come out to dinner with me tonight?"

"I would relish a chance to catch up, but I am to dine with Stoker, the manager, tonight. We are to discuss the play's performance and further promotion.

You are welcome to join us, but I fear that all the business talk would bore you."

"Not at all. That is, if you are sure that I am not intruding."

"Certainly not. We would be most pleased to have you with us. Now, just let me finish getting changed and I'll be with you."

Lazarus left Mansfield in his dressing room and hung around the stage door, watching the stage hands and gas men pack up for the night. All of the artistes had already left. Eventually Mansfield emerged, looking much more composed than he had been moments previously. He wore his dinner suit with a white cravat and well-polished boots.

"Ah, you have met my associate Mr. Stoker, Lazarus?"

"Yes," Lazarus replied as the theatre manager came over to them. "I introduced myself earlier."

"Bram here is the finest house manager in all England," Mansfield said. "And also an accomplished writer."

"A hobby at present," said Stoker.

"A hobby with encouraging prospects! And my good friend Lazarus Longman here is a world-famous explorer."

"Yes, I do remember reading something of your exploits in the papers," Stoker said. "Something to do with Great Zimbabwe?"

"That's right," said Lazarus.

"That's just the tip of his exploits," Mansfield went on. "He's been to India, the Americas and Egypt too, if I'm not mistaken?"

"Egypt?" Stoker said, his eyebrows raised. "You intrigue me, sir. "I have a good friend who has been many times. Brought back all sorts of jewels and mummies. Is it true that their religion involved the resurrection of the dead?"

"Well not as such," said Lazarus. "It's a common misconception."

"Oh, I don't mean mummies walking around as you or I do, I speak metaphorically of course. I refer to reincarnation."

"Mummies walking around?" Mansfield said with a snort of laughter. "You see, Lazarus, Bram here has a feverish and demented imagination. One never knows what fantasy he's going to dream up next."

Lazarus forced a smile. "Shall we be off? I'm famished."

Chapter Three

In which our hero is introduced to a new acquaintance

The following morning, Lazarus returned to Whitehall and met Morton in the long corridor outside his office. An Otis hydraulic lift took them down to a cellar deep below street level.

Morton caught him gazing at the brick pillars and arches that looked Tudor at the very latest. "Never been down here, eh? It's where we keep our tinkerers, tailors and quartermasters, not to mention the armory and rifle range."

"You said I was to meet my associate," Lazarus said. "Is he one of your 'tinkerers'?"

"Not at all. I just wanted you both to get some practice in on the targets. Never know when it might come in handy during your plumbing of the depths of the East End."

"I can assure you that my aim is as true as ever."

"Well it's just a good idea for you both to fire off a few rounds side by side. Develops a bond, you know."

"Will I be getting another Colt Starblazer?"

Morton sucked air in between his teeth. "Not really inconspicuous is it, a shiny new model like that? No, I think we'll give you something older, perhaps military issue. Firearms are certainly not uncommon in the circles you will be moving in, but you need something that rings true to your cover story."

"And that is?"

"Ex-soldier. Fought in the Soudan but was injured. Now you're just looking for good honest work. Strong man, good with your hands. Warehouse work, that sort of thing. Those are the places that these socialist groups tend to spring from."

They entered a large cellar with brick arches on either side. Several scientific-looking men in frock coats were dwarfed by perhaps the largest man Lazarus had ever seen. His rough flannel jacket strained against bulging shoulders that started a good foot above the head of the tallest scientist present. A tattered waistcoat met sagging grey trousers patched at the knees. A flat cap was jammed on his head; a head which was the most remarkable thing about him, for no part of his face was visible. Instead, a mask of tin or some other metal had been fashioned into the likeness of a square-jawed mug complete with eyeholes, nostrils and a black oval between open lips, into which the man kept jamming the end of a fat cigar before exhaling blasts of smoke.

"Lazarus, meet your colleague for the duration of the case. His real name is withheld for reasons of security but the chaps down here call him Mr. Clumps."

"H... how do you do?" Lazarus stammered, holding out his hand to the imposing figure.

The man grasped it in a gloved fist, but his grip was surprisingly gentle as he shook it. "Pleased to meet you, Mr. Longman," said the voice behind the mask. "I've heard a great deal about you."

Well, he was polite enough, that was something at least. Lazarus was put in mind of an oversized simpleton from a Dickens novel, but couldn't remember which one.

"Poor Mr. Clumps here suffers from phossy jaw after working for many years manufacturing warning flares for the navy," Morton explained. "His face is ruined by the exposure to white phosphorus, and he feels the need to hide it for the sake of decency. Now, I'd like you both to get reacquainted with the firearms in our arsenal. The rifle range is just through those doors there."

They went through the double doors and Lazarus immediately knew how Mr. Clumps had got his name. His wide, flat feet were encased in what could only be custom-made boots, thudding down with resounding 'clumps' that reverberated throughout the cellar. He walked with a shuffling, lopsided gait that reminded Lazarus of something he couldn't quite put his finger on. In the room beyond, they found targets set up and a table with an array of pistols and boxes of ammunition.

Lazarus spotted a Colt Peacemaker, a Smith and Wesson Model 3 Russian – *Katarina's gun of choice...* – a British Bulldog pocket revolver, a Webley Mk I and his own preferred Enfield Mark II. He picked up the Peacemaker first, being the forerunner to the state of the art Starblazer. He loaded cartridges into the cylinder, leaving one chamber empty, and fired them off in quick succession at his target.

The cracks of the rounds echoed along the length of the range. Splinters of wood and shredded paper that had been plastered to the target drifted in the wake of the shots. The smell of gun smoke brought back memories of bloody warfare in the African grasslands, and the stink of intrigue and clandestine killings from his work with the bureau.

"Top marks, Longman," said Morton, taking his fingers out of his ears. "All five on the target. Try the Webley. We drew up the contract for ten thousand of them last year. The loading mechanism is a vast improvement on the Enfield's."

"I'd like to see Mr. Clumps have a try," said Lazarus.

The big man brought his cigar up to his silver lips and inhaled deeply, blowing the smoke out through his mask's nostrils. He selected the Webley Mk I and broke it open to slide in the cartridges. Lazarus watched him intently while reloading the Peacemaker. As Mr. Clumps raised the revolver and pointed it at the target, Lazarus aimed his Peacemaker at the big man's head.

"Drop it!" he shouted. "All of you get back!" he commanded Morton and the scientists.

Mr. Clump's metallic face slowly revolved on its neck to fix its hollow eyes on Lazarus. His gun arm lowered but still gripped the Webley.

"Longman, have you lost your bloody mind?" Morton bellowed.

"Stay back!" Lazarus shouted. "I don't know what's going on or how it happened, but this thing is a mechanical! Somehow a bloody mechanical posing as a human has snuck into your top secret basement, Morton!"

"You may put down your revolver, Mr. Clumps," Morton said, "lest our agent actually damage you."

Mr. Clumps set the Webley down on the table and turned to face Lazarus.

"Bravo, Longman," Morton said. "Bravo. I was confident that if anybody could call him out on it, then it was you. Ingenious workmanship, eh? You can set your gun down too, you know. He's not a danger."

"Morton, what the hell is going on?" said Lazarus, still pointing his gun at those blank, lifeless eyes.

"I'm sorry for the trick, old boy, but we needed to see just how passable our creation here is. It seems that only a man with extensive experience with these mechanicals can see through its disguise. Still, that's good enough for us."

"You mean your crackpots actually *built* one of these things? How?"

"With some help from our American friends. We called in some specialists from the C.S.A. for advice, but he's all British workmanship. Put down your gun and I'll show you."

Lazarus slowly set the pistol down on the table, not taking his eyes off the mechanical.

"Mr. Clumps," said Morton. "Remove your mask."

The giant reached up and fiddled with some screws that were disguised in the molded sideburns of the mask. With those steady, massive hands, he removed the metal visage to reveal what had once been a man's head. It was sickly, pale and bald. Its jaw was missing and a blackened pipe protruded from the esophagus.

"The organic pilot's vocal chords are still intact, which was essential for authentic speech," Morton explained. "Steam from its internal boiler is released from this pipe too, disguised as cigar smoke which necessitates the permanent 'smoking' action. It's a fake cigar, of course, with a small light that simulates burning and a scent valve that disguises the steam as tobacco smoke. A mild blend from Spitalfields, in fact."

"What of its fuel source?" Lazarus asked. "Not mechanite, surely."

"Actually, yes," Morton replied with a smile.

"How on earth did you get mechanite into England?"

"It was part of a new deal with the C.S.A. They lent us some scientists and a small supply of the stuff in order for us to try out this experimental model. Think, Longman! Think if we could disguise mechanicals as people!"

"To what end? They're not clever enough to be spies. And too clumsy to be assassins."

"Ah, yes, well, their applications are not yet fully understood, but it's through experimentation that we shall find out the potential possibilities."

To Lazarus this sounded a lot like 'we built it because we could'. "And this is supposed to be my colleague on the mission? A mechanical? Well you can forget it. I'm out if this thing has anything to do with it."

"Come now, Longman, don't be prejudiced."

"Prejudiced? Several of these things tried to kill me in Egypt. And I've seen the unfortunate prototypes this kind of research turns out. Men assimilated against their will, mutilated, corrupted. I don't stand for this and I'm surprised you do, Morton."

"The world is changing, Lazarus. We have enemies gathering around us like a storm cloud that threatens to engulf Europe, or even the world. We need to keep current with progress lest our rivals surpass us."

"It's not just my moral stance on the matter that's the problem. This mission is an undercover job. How long do you think I'll last in the East End with this great lug following me around? A seven foot mechanical powered by an illegal energy source? Very bloody inconspicuous!"

"Doesn't he pass for human? An extraordinary

human to be sure, but you yourself did not know him for what he was at first."

"I had my suspicions."

"How *did* you know, in fact?"

"It was when he aimed his pistol. Mechanicals have a certain way of holding a gun. They don't take aim like us, slow and coordinated with a relaxed elbow and a firm grip. Mechanicals thrust the gun out like a brand, their arm stiff as a plank."

Morton frowned. "I see. You boys listening to this?"

The scientists nodded.

"But as I said, you have come into contact with these things before. You know how they work and how to spot them. Nobody in the East End will. And this is why I wanted you in particular for this case. We need somebody to keep an eye on Mr. Clumps here when he's out and about on his first mission. A test drive, as it were."

"So I'm a nanny for a mechanical."

"Think of yourselves more as a duo. He is there to protect you, and you are there to make the best use you can of him. There's more riding on this mission than just finding out what the socialists are up to."

"I still don't like it."

"You'll complement each other very well, I feel. As I've said before, you are one of our best agents. And Mr. Clumps is damn near invulnerable, not to mention incredibly strong. You'll be safe as houses. Now, would you like us to arrange accommodation for you both? It won't be Langham Hotel standards, naturally, but you'll need a base of operations and somewhere to get your head down at night."

"Best if I arrange accommodation," Lazarus said. "I

know the East End and I don't want you boys putting me up in some doss house."

That afternoon Lazarus took the opportunity to pay a visit to his mysterious cobbler in Stepney. Who knew when he would have a chance to pursue his personal interests while he was ferreting around the gutters on Morton's orders?

57 Copley Street may well have been a cobblers at one point. There was a sign above the door indicating that at least, but the windows were grimy and weeds grew between the cracks in the steps that led up to its battered and flaking front door. He peered through one of the windows and saw nothing but gloom and cobwebs. He knocked on the door.

After waiting for an amount of time that told him he was not going to receive an answer, he wandered around the back and scrambled over a wooden fence. It was all very strange. Why leave a calling card for a business that no longer existed? Either somebody was trying to throw him off the scent or wanted him here for some other reason. He found himself in a shabby yard filled with bricks and broken furniture. The back door was bolted but the window to the side was slightly open, which was handy.

Too handy.

He scrambled in and drew his Enfield revolver. This whole business was fishy enough to call for caution. The ground floor of the house was empty. He found only peeling wallpaper and a marked workbench littered with tools rusted beyond use. He climbed the stairs slowly, trying not to make them creak too much.

The bedrooms were as deserted as the rooms below, but as he entered the last one a boot lashed out from behind the door and caught his wrist, sending the revolver skittering across the floorboards.

He whirled to face his attacker and found an oriental sort bearing down on him, with a flurry of kicks and punches that Lazarus desperately blocked, recognizing the martial art at once. It was *Muay*, the fighting style of Siam, and not a style that he himself was wholly unfamiliar with.

He lunged forward and gripped his attacker in a neck hold, flinging his legs back alternately to dodge the savage knee blows to his abdomen. Using all the strength in his body, he hurled the man to the ground but had overestimated his opponent's weight and found himself toppling over to land by his side. Then, it was a frantic scramble to be the first man to his feet. The more agile oriental was up first and swung his leg around at head height, connecting with Lazarus's temple with a dizzying crack that sent him sprawling once more.

Lazarus had kept himself in shape and occasionally practiced the moves he had learned in childhood, but he knew he was no match for this mysterious attacker who no doubt trained several hours a day. He sprung to his feet as fast as he could, ready to block the next kick which he just about managed. He ducked low and punched with his left but was blocked, then brought up his right knee, also blocked. An elbow came crashing down on his forehead which sent sparks flashing before his eyes. He reeled backwards, protecting his head with his bunched fists. He tasted blood.

Damn me! he thought. There was no way he could

beat this fellow or even escape, for that matter. He had to use his head—metaphorically speaking, of course. Why was this mad foreigner attacking him? To kill him? Or to merely knock him unconscious? Either way, the only method of surviving a potentially fatal beating was to cede to the man's demands. *But it has to look real.*

He dodged and weaved, waiting for the right moment. As the attacker brought his knee up in a violent head attack, Lazarus rolled with it, letting it connect with his cheekbone as softly as possible.

It was not nearly as soft as he would have liked. His skull felt like it had been split apart like a watermelon under a sledgehammer. It didn't take much acting to fall back and collapse on the floor. The real act of deception came when the pain, searing and hot, throbbed through his face and brain as he lay still, feigning unconsciousness.

The oriental remained light on his feet, but peered over Lazarus's prostrate form. Lazarus had closed his eyes so he did not see what sort of expression—pride, curiosity or stone cold professionalism—was passing over his victor's face. Apparently satisfied, the man backed out of the room and shut the door behind him. A key turned in the lock.

Lazarus opened his eyes a crack and found that his left one was fast swelling shut. He could hear the sound of the man's footsteps descending the stairs. This was a rum business. Why knock him unconscious only to lock him in an upstairs room? He could hear movement below as the foreigner clattered about. He waited until all was still before rising.

The room spun. His brain screamed and his tender prodding to see if his cheekbone was still in once piece brought tears to his eyes. It was not shattered, so that was something. He breathed deeply and tried to dispel the feeling of grogginess. There was a strange scent, like something burning. An effect of the trauma his head had received? He sniffed the air. Something was indeed burning, and he had a good idea that it was the house he was in.

So that was the plan! Lure him here to this deserted dump, knock him unconscious and then burn the house down with him in it. A tragic accident, or so the police report would read. But why? Who had he so grievously offended that they should want him dead? The purchaser of the journal? He chided himself for speculating when he was in imminent danger, for the crackle of the blaze was audible now.

The door was locked. That left the window. He slid it open and peered out into the street below. The drop wouldn't kill him. But it might break a leg, possibly two, and that was to be avoided if at all possible. He looked around the room. It was empty. No useful bed sheets that might be knotted together, no mattress to hurl out to cushion his landing. Smoke was creeping in under the door. If he could only get through it, he could make it to the rooms at the rear and see if there wasn't something there that might be of aid to him. *But how?*

Had he his gun he might have shot out the lock, but of course the cursed man had taken it with him. He booted the door. It was an old door and the wooden panel he had struck gave a little. He booted it again, as hard as he could. The paint cracked, hinting at a flexibility in the old wood. He kicked again and again, imagining it was the oriental's face and this was payback for the beating he had just taken.

The wood cracked. Another blow allowed his foot out into the corridor, through a splintered hole that scraped his shin. He retrieved his leg gingerly and began working at the wood around the hole he had made. It came away in splinters and soon he was able to scramble out into the smoke-filled corridor.

He coughed and hacked. An orange glow illuminated the stairwell. Shielding his face, he crossed the landing, entered one of the other bedrooms and shoved open the window. He thrust his head out and gulped down fresh air. Within his reach was a drainpipe painted black. He clambered out of the window and grabbed hold of it, finding a foothold for one leg, then the other.

There was a grating sound as the fixtures protested at his weight. He began to descend and had barely managed a foot before the drainpipe loosened itself and began to drift away from the wall. His fists seized it in a death grip as he fell seemingly in slow motion. He just had time to turn his head to see what he might be landing on, before the bush was flattened beneath him and his shoulder struck the wooden fence. It gave a little and he came to rest on solid ground, spitting earth and clawing at the tangles of foliage in his eyes.

He got to his feet and watched the flames through the grimy windows as they ate away at the walls and ceiling, rising up to consume the top floor of the house.

Chapter Four

In which Limehouse offers several clues

The bureau had found them jobs in a warehouse that let directly onto Shadwell Basin. It was a proper contract that meant they avoided the casual 'call-on' which had prospective laborers herded up like cattle at a market to be picked for a day's work by a foreman, only to be cast aside when they were no longer needed.

As Lazarus and Mr. Clumps sat down in the office of the manager, Lazarus realized that they must look like the worst couple of rogues. His left eye was still badly swollen and his lip was cut, courtesy of his mysterious Siamese gentleman. His companion looked like, well, a gorilla wearing a theatrical mask.

The manager looked at them over his broad desk, a certain expression of distaste curling his features. "What's with the metal mug?"

"Phossy jaw," Lazarus explained.

"Can he speak for himself?"

"Yes, sir," said Mr. Clumps in his soft tones. "Phossy jaw. From the navy factories."

"You don't want to see him with it off," Lazarus advised.

The manager frowned. "You've both been recommended to me by a mutual friend," he said. "I run a tight operation here. Goods come in, we unpack 'em, store 'em, re-pack 'em and ship 'em out. That's more or less the gist of it. I want hard work from my employees and no slacking. You lads look like strong fellas but have you got ethics, that's what I'm wondering."

"Oh, yes," Lazarus answered. "Ethics by the barrel load. You'll have nothing from us but good honest work."

"Glad to hear it. Go with Tappy here, he'll show you what's what."

Tappy was a skinny man in a flat cap who loitered by the doorway with a small dog-end hanging off his bottom lip. "Got a shipment lined up for you already," he said and led them out onto the docks where a vessel from Ceylon was moored.

They were put to work with another couple of workers, shifting crates of tea from the ship's derrick. The work was hard and fast and Lazarus soon felt the need to remove his cap and roll his shirtsleeves up. He was sticky with sweat and within two hours had developed a new sense of respect for the stamina of dockworkers. Mr. Clumps carried on, taking crate after crate on his own, without breaking his stride or even removing his coat, much to the admiration of their new colleagues. Lazarus decided he would have to have a word with him about appearances.

"Your mate's a quiet one," Tappy said during a quick tea break. They were sitting on some empty crates in the sun. Mr. Clumps had his back to them as he looked out over Shadwell Basin. "Strong, though. I can't complain."

"Shy, honest sort," Lazarus replied, wiping the sweat from his brow with his cap. "Known him a couple of months and he hasn't said much else to me but 'good morning'. Still, I never could stand a chatterbox."

He watched Mr. Clumps staring at the flat body of water, his massive cigar slowly glowing away while he puffed out clouds of scented steam. He still had on his coat. Lazarus gulped down the lukewarm tea. How they were going to get away with all this was beyond his comprehension.

The days trickled by. Lazarus grew immensely frustrated at the time it was taking to find anything out. His colleagues were likeable enough, if a little rough. Many were foreigners; Poles, Germans, Irish. They had a coarse humor and several of them were clearly heavy drinkers. One or two petty crooks. But none were the hardened revolutionists wanting to overthrow the social order that he was looking for. Most of them could barely read, and he imagined that they wouldn't know Karl Marx from Lottie Collins.

On top of it all he was so tired from lifting, carrying and hauling things about that his very bones ached. He had hacked his way through jungles, trailed across the blazing desert with an empty canteen and fought the Ashanti warriors tooth and nail on strict rations, but even he found the daily grind of a dockside worker almost too much. Every night he would crash down on the cot in their lodgings in Limehouse and sleep like an old drunk, snoring away while Mr. Clumps sat in the only chair in the room, his mechanite furnace slowly ticking over and the glowing end of his cigar going up and down as he exhaled through the night—not sleeping, but watching and waiting.

Lazarus was responsible for keeping Mr. Clumps up and running. The bureau had supplied him with a quantity of mechanite which he kept wrapped in an oilskin beneath a loose floorboard in their room. It seemed absurd to keep such a valuable trove in such an unassuming and seedy location with only a flimsy wooden door and his own British Bulldog pocket revolver to defend it. But nobody was looking for it, and even if some lowlife managed to prize it from his possession they likely wouldn't know it from a few chunks of schist.

Lazarus had not given up his private concerns, and in the slow wait for information on the socialist groups that may or may not have infested the warehouses of Shadwell Docks, he had time to pursue them, even if he was dog tired. One Sunday afternoon he decided that it was time to pay the old lime oast Mansfield had mentioned a visit.

Rows upon rows of tiny worker's cottages lined the canals of one of London's worst slums. Dilapidated barges rested upon the mud, awaiting the evening tide. Public houses and opium dens were common, and shabby-looking children played with mangy dogs in the streets. Rising up above all of this were the conical lime oasts that lent the district its name. Several were still in use, but a great many were empty shells with broken windows and crumbling chimneys, their fires long left untended.

Lazarus had come alone. Mr. Clumps had expressed a surprising degree of trepidation at allowing his superior to wander off alone on this overcast Sunday afternoon, but Lazarus had insisted. He was a private man, and when they were not pursuing their mission's goals he must be allowed some private time. Perhaps he had family he wanted to visit, or a lady friend who missed him. These were things that the steam-man could never understand, Lazarus explained, and Mr.

Clumps did an alarming impression of a man sulking when he had left him sitting on his chair in their lodgings.

As Lazarus made his way across the weed-ravaged yard towards the address Mansfield had given him, his footsteps echoed across the cracked concrete, reverberating off the red brickwork of the surrounding buildings. He looked up at the lime oast with its dark eye-like windows of broken glass and conical kiln looming over him. He patted his coat pocket instinctively, feeling the shape of the Bulldog revolver. The smallness of it made him feel uneasy. He missed the reassuring bulge of his Enfield and especially the heavy weight of his Starblazer.

The main door was secured with heavy, rusted chains, so he followed the building around to the left, looking for another entrance. He came across a small wooden door that was barely hanging from its hinges. He pushed it aside and he stepped in.

Some pigeons, startled by his entrance, burst upwards in a flurry of feathers and out through a gaping hole in the roof. The place was dim. All about were scattered the remnants of the kiln's former life. Worker's tools, rusted and filthy, lay strewn on ancient benches and a thick layer of dust and grime coated everything. At the far end of the building, the floor dropped away to a set of slime-encrusted steps leading to the water. It had once been used as a small dock and now a thick layer of scum sat on the water, obscuring its depths.

He poked around a little more, but to no avail. If anything had been amiss here, then someone had since removed all trace. It didn't look like it had been used for anything since its fires cooled, many years ago.

Disappointed, he left the building and made his way back across the yard.

Some children were playing on an old heap of broken masonry and looked a little startled to see him emerge from the lime oast. There were four in all, three boys and a girl, all dressed in shabby jackets and caps.

"Oi, mister!" shouted one. "Are you a copper?"

"Nope," Lazarus replied, walking past them.

"I'll bet you are. I'll bet you're investigating ghosts," the lad said.

"Why would a copper care two pennies about ghosts?" Lazarus asked. "Not that I am a copper. And what's all this about ghosts, anyway?"

"Cos a ghost lives in there," the boy replied. "I seen it."

"What did you see?" Lazarus asked.

The boy wiped the back of his hand across his nose and sniffed. "Well, it weren't really me," he admitted. "It was me brother Ben. He saw it late at night, a real ghost it was. It was all dressed in black and floated over the ground."

"Your brother's been on the gin," said the girl. "Seein' things."

"S'all a load of cobblers anyway!" exclaimed another of their companions. "It ain't no ghost. My dad saw him in daylight and he weren't floating. My dad reckons its Todd."

"Todd?" Lazarus enquired. "Who's he?"

"Everyone's heard of old Sweeney Todd," exclaimed the second boy incredulously. "He's the Demon Barber of Fleet Street. He invites people into his shop for a shave and then he cuts their throat with his razor. Then he sells their bodies to a woman what makes 'em into meat pies!"

"Good grief!" Lazarus said. "Where do you hear such things?"

"Everyone's heard of ol' Todd," he repeated. "Ask anyone. That's his lair where he hides from the coppers."

Lazarus had heard enough. He left the children to their playing and headed back towards his lodgings. On the way, he thought long and hard about his encounter with the street urchins. They may have let their imaginations run away with them, but one thing was for certain; *someone* had been going in and out of the old lime oast.

During those dull, exhausting days, Lazarus also found time to enquire of Limehouse's Asian population if anybody knew of the recent arrival of a man from Siam. Limehouse had its share of Buddhist temples and he surmised that his attacker, if he were a true Siamese, would likely be a Buddhist, and if so would undoubtedly visit some temple in the area for his devotions.

The Chinese population of Limehouse had grown in recent years. Tea and opium merchants from Shanghai and Tianjin sought homes and business opportunities amidst the chandlers and rope makers. Cantonese sailors, marooned by shipping lines that offered no return journeys to their deckhands, were left to build new lives for themselves in London's dockside communities. Stalls and shops had sprung up to cater to the new settlers, selling dried foods, herbs and medicinal remedies while gambling dens and oriental restaurants clustered together in the narrow streets.

It took several days of asking around before he was told by one Chinese man that yes, a number of tough Siamese men had been seen frequenting a temple on

Pennyfields. It surprised Lazarus and unnerved him to think that his would-be assassin was not alone. He had already surmised that the man must be working for somebody higher up who held a grudge against him. It then stood to reason that this individual had several Siamese fighters in his employ. And to find the snake's head, they say, one must follow its tail.

He watched the temple on Pennyfields for several evenings, and finally spotted his man emerging from the unremarkable building of plum-colored brick. It was most definitely the same man; those loose-fitting clothes that suggested a previous trade at sea and the smooth, nut-brown face unadorned with beard or moustache. He grabbed a nearby street urchin and pointed the man out.

"See that man?" he asked the child who blinked up at him, unsure if he was going to be given a farthing or a thick ear. "How would you like to earn half a crown?"

The boy's eyes goggled at the prospect.

"I want you to follow that man, not now, he's too far gone, but he'll be back. I want to know where he goes and who he sees. If he stops at a house I want the address. I don't care if he trails you all over London. If he takes a cab, I want you to keep on it. I've seen you lads do that, right?"

"Right!" nodded the boy, his peaked cap wagging up and down.

"Half a crown. Here's sixpence for the time being. I'll be back on Sunday for your news."

Still nodding vigorously, the child went on his way, giddy with his new employment. Lazarus hadn't the time to spend any more evenings and weekends waiting and watching but London's hordes of unwashed, illiterate and abandoned urchins was a more effective grapevine than anything the metropolitan or municipal police forces could muster between them. His lad would turn up the goods, he had no doubt about that.

Chapter Five

In which the journal is obtained

The daily grind of working life in the big city was taking its toll on Lazarus. He was a man who had spent most of his life either in exotic places or in a library reading about them. The past was what fascinated him, with all its colors and infinite lives entwined along paths of mysticism and strange faiths. The grey, gloomy drudgery of the industrial age and its modern rationalism was a terrible drag on his soul. He felt hopelessly out of his depth in his mission, not least because there seemed so very few leads open to him.

Then, by a twist of fortune, Lazarus was brought into contact with a man who might just have the connections he desired. It was on Tuesday that Lazarus and Mr. Clumps were told by Tappy that they would be better suited—owing to Mr. Clumps's massive strength—to loading the carts that left the warehouse. It was harder work than unloading the derricks, as it involved heaving large crates and sacks up onto the back of the carts while their drivers stood idly by smoking their pipes.

Lazarus found himself despairing even more at this new burden on his already waning strength, and was cursing his companion for his efficiency when he discovered that the majority of the men who did the tougher jobs in the warehouse were Jews of Polish or

Russian extraction.

There was a distinct anti-Semitic streak in most of the workers, and so it stood to reason that the real back-breaking labor fell upon the shoulders of the Jews whose very existence caused their colleagues to despise them for taking jobs that might have otherwise gone to Englishmen.

Lazarus did his best to strike up friendly conversation with them and found himself rebuffed on a number of occasions. Distrust, it seemed, came from both sides. But there was one fellow who did not seem as reluctant to converse with him.

His name was Kovalev. He was an elderly Russian with rough hands and a stooped back that suggested many years of backbreaking labor. His English was good and he possessed a vocabulary far beyond those of Lazarus's fellow countrymen in the rest of the warehouse. This made Lazarus think of him as one of the many educated Jews who, pushed out of their homeland by pogroms and the hate of their countrymen, found themselves diminished to physical labor in London's East End.

Their conversations never drifted into the realm of politics. Lazarus was reluctant to push them in that direction, lest Kovalev grow suspicious as to his reasons. He decided that he would have to bait him and see if the old Russian, or anybody else for that matter, might be drawn into a discussion that would reveal their political standings. He had the bait in the form of a copy of the Commonweal; the official journal of the Socialist League that he carried around in his jacket pocket. All he needed was the opportunity to reveal his taste in literature to his colleagues. He developed a plan to do just that.

That Sunday Lazarus spent the afternoon awaiting the appearance of his street urchin on Pennyfields. He sniffed down the scent of opium that drifted from a nearby open window and remembered his days in New York with Mansfield, wallowing in dens very much like these ones. One Chinatown was very much like another the world over, he concluded.

Eventually the boy he sought rounded the corner, his hands shoved deep into his pockets. He saw Lazarus and beamed as if relieved that his patron had actually showed up.

"Well, lad?" he asked him. "Good news?"

"Oh, yes, sir! Your man turned up all right and I followed him all over." He then proceeded to give Lazarus a long list of the gambling dens and cafes the fellow had visited, along with multiple visits to a lodging house two streets over. Lazarus wrote it all down on a small notepad. It seemed fairly run-of-the-mill stuff; the expected routine of many denizens of Limehouse and Shadwell. Then the lad reeled off an address of a none-too-shabby town house in Bloomsbury.

"Bloomsbury?" Lazarus asked, raising his eyebrow at the boy. "Bit out of the way for our fellow, isn't it?"

"Ain't 'alf! He took an hansom and I had to switch growler three times to keep a mince on him! I thought he was going all the way to Westminster!"

"This house, what is it like?"

"A right toff's gaff. High windows and ivy and all."

"Was he admitted through the front door?"

"You must be joking! He snuck around the back to

the tradesmen's entrance."

"See anybody else about? A butler or something?"

"Nah, he slipped in too quick for me to catch a butchers."

"Well, my lad you've earned your half crown." Lazarus dug into his pocket.

"Half?" the boy exclaimed. "You said an 'ole crown!"

"I said half. And that was in addition to the sixpence I gave you last week, but nice try. Now hoppit before I give you a toe in the arse."

"Much obliged, sir," the lad replied, making the half a crown vanish into his clothes and then himself vanish into the crowded street.

Lazarus returned to Shadwell and whiled away the afternoon with Mr. Clumps. The big fellow had taken to reading newspapers. Lazarus was not only surprised by the mechanical's ability to read but by his interest and understanding of the articles within. The pubs being shut, Lazarus fished out a bottle of gin he had purchased and sat on the bed drinking from a chipped tumbler. He offered his companion some.

"No, thank you," Mr. Clumps replied.

"Can you process alcohol?" Lazarus asked him. He had seen him eat and drink when the need required it. It was not essential, for his furnace was the only energy source the mechanical required. Clumps had been discreet about how he deposited any bodily waste, a discretion Lazarus was rather grateful for.

"I can drink just about anybody under the table," Mr. Clumps replied. "I believe that's the expression."

"Very good," Lazarus said. Conversations with the mechanical were not exactly stimulating and he decided that perhaps, head for drink or no, his only bottle of

Madam Geneva would be wasted on a mechanical. Not for the first time since beginning this assignment, he found himself missing human companionship.

When dusk approached, Lazarus walked to Commercial Road and took a hansom to Bloomsbury. Being a Sunday evening, the house's occupants—whoever they may be—would most likely be in. But the cover of night was essential to what he had in mind and occupied or not, he wanted to see the home of whoever it was that wanted him dead.

The red brick three-storied houses facing parks and tree-lined squares were the peaceful seclusions of London's authors and poets. Behind lace curtains and velvet drapes they enjoyed candle-lit suppers and literary circles. Lazarus knew that behind at least one of these serene, well-kept houses, dwelt a would-be murderer.

The driver pulled up at the address. Lazarus paid him and walked around to the back, where the tradesman's entrance was screened by a brick wall. The tops of bushes poked up from the other side, and Lazarus smiled at the easy opportunity for a housebreaker. Not that he was one, but it amounted to the same thing in the eyes of the law. After checking that nobody was taking an evening stroll down the back lanes, he scrambled up and over the wall and into the neat garden beyond.

Lights were on in all the ground floor rooms and in only one of the first-floor rooms. There was no drainpipe (and had there been any he would have only used it as a last resort, owing to his recent misadventure with one). No other form of entry to the upper floors presented itself. There was, however, a cellar-flap with a padlock. Lazarus had expected as much and had brought a set of skeleton keys for such a job.

It took a good deal of fiddling to spring the lock, but at last it came away and he silently lifted the flap and descended into the cellar. Rows of jars on shelves glinted in the light from the hatch. Pickles, jams, compots and other relishes twinkled between boxes of tea, tins of tongue and potted meats. He fumbled around and found a door—bolted.

He drew his penknife and slid it in the jamb, lifting the latch with the barest of 'clinks'. The kitchen beyond was deserted, apart from a fat old cook snoring softly in an armchair, her mob cap over her eyes and half a glass of sherry resting on the arm. Lazarus snuck out and ducked into the shadows of a passageway, narrowly avoiding detection by the scullery maid who came downstairs bearing a tray of empty glasses.

Upon reaching the hallway at the top of the stairs, he could hear voices—foreign voices. The door to the drawing room was ajar. Although he could see nobody, he could hear a man speaking what he recognized as Siamese from the familiar throat of a fellow Englishman.

The language that had once been his only form of communication came more than a little slowly to him these days. It had been many years since he had mouthed the many tones and monosyllables of Siam and he struggled to follow the conversation.

He guessed that the Englishman was the master of the house and, if the master was giving instructions to his followers in the drawing room, then his study would undoubtedly be unoccupied. He made for the stairs and took them two at a time, but with gentle footsteps lest any creak beneath the oriental carpet give him away.

As he suspected, the master's study was the room on the first floor with the light burning. He slipped inside and found himself in a veritable museum of the orient. Green glazed ceramics from the Sukhothai kingdom, bronze figures of multi-limbed Hindoo deities and statuettes of Buddha, wicked-bladed weapons of the Khmer Empire and solid bronze elephant bells decorated the shelves, interspersed with leather bound tomes on the Ayutthaya Kingdom, Angkor and the Mon, Tai and Malay peoples.

Lazarus went straight to the desk where a green shaded lamp illuminated a spread of documents, notes and maps all pertaining to Siam and the surrounding kingdoms. He would have loved to have perused them at leisure and ascertain who his mysterious fellow enthusiast was and what his intentions were, but his eyes fell on a small, leather-bound journal that lay to one side.

It was a battered and weathered old thing, bulging against the string tied around it that kept its loose contents together. A simple metal clasp had once sufficed, but was now broken. He untied the string, trying to keep his hands steady, strongly suspecting that this was the very journal he chased. It fell open in his hands and he began leafing through the papers. Faded photographs of temples and natives met his eyes, as well as sketches of plants and small creatures. The journal itself was a small collection of loose papers written in a neat, cursive hand. He searched for a name, and his heart skipped a beat when he came across it.

Thomas Spencer Tyndall.

A foot fell on the stairs and Lazarus looked up. His time was up, but he wasn't leaving without the journal. Another problem was how to escape, for the window was too high to jump and if he went out onto the landing he would be seen. He was trapped. He looked down at the papers on the desk and tried desperately to think of a solution.

The master of the house stepped into the study and his eyes widened with astonishment at the intruder, before dulling to a silent anger. He was about the same age as Lazarus, but blond with shoulder-length hair, thick and golden. His skin was very pale. If he had ever been to any of the places he was so interested in, Lazarus decided that he probably spent all of his time under the shade of a parasol.

"So you've got a bit of gumption eh, Longman?" said the man. "Not to mention an infuriating habit of survival."

"You seem to have me at a disadvantage," said Lazarus. "Perhaps you'd like to introduce yourself and explain why you tried to have me killed. And what is your interest in Tyndall's journal?"

"The name's Constantine Westcott. I can allow you to know that much out of courtesy, but the rest is hardly relevant as your time on this earth is short. You really are a bloody nuisance." He called down in Siamese and there came the sound of at least two pairs of feet hurrying up the stairs.

Two oriental faces appeared on either side of Westcott's head. Lazarus recognized one of them as the man who had left him for dead in a burning house. He looked as surprised as his employer had been at seeing Lazarus alive.

Westcott looked down at the journal in Lazarus's hands. "I'll be taking that back, thank you very much."

The two thugs advanced. Lazarus seized the lamp from the desk and swung it at the head of the first man who got near. The man ducked it and swung his fist into Lazarus's gut, making him double over. The journal fell from his hands. The second man seized it and passed it to Westcott while the first attacker—Lazarus's friend from before—landed blow after blow on him, alternating his left and right fists.

Lazarus tried to block and dodge, but the ferocious tempo of the man indicated that he was expressing his frustrations at having failed to kill him the first time.

"All right, that's enough," said Westcott in Siamese.

Lazarus gasped for air. He was lying on the carpet, his left hand gripping the corner of the desk. Blood trickled from his nose and between his lips. His ears rang.

"Get him upstairs," said Westcott. "And don't let any of my household see him. They're suspicious enough about what goes on here. I'll be up in a few minutes and then we shall put an end to Mr. Lazarus Longman once and for all."

The Siamese men grabbed Lazarus under the armpits and after hauling him to his feet, dragged him from the room. The carpeted stairs banged against his knees and toes as they took him up first one flight and then up a second set, leading to the attic.

A bare room with a single chair in the centre awaited him. Several boxes covered in sheets loomed like ghosts in the shadows. A small window was set in the slanted ceiling, and through it Lazarus could see that it had started to rain. Fat drops drummed on the glass, making the dark little room seem totally isolated from the outside world. Opposite the window was a small door set into the brick wall that Lazarus assumed led to the water cistern.

Lazarus was shoved roughly into the chair. While

one of the men stood guard by the door through which they had come, the other began rummaging around in a battered leather chest for some rope with which to bind their captive.

Lazarus wasn't about to let himself get tied to a chair for the pleasure of anyone, and so was on his feet in an instant, grabbing his chair by its back and swinging it with all his might onto the head of the man by the door.

The chair splintered into fragments and Lazarus jammed his knee into the man's groin as an added weakener. The man at the chest came charging towards them and Lazarus turned, gripping his man in a neck hold, and hurled him into his accomplice. The two men went sprawling and Lazarus made for the door that held the cistern.

He had an idea that, as in many terraced London houses, the attics of all in the row were connected by a long corridor. This had been remarked upon in the papers as a dangerously easy opportunity for burglars and, in his current predicament, he desperately hoped that it was the case here.

He flung open the door and squeezed himself behind the cistern, peering into the gloom. He thanked his stars to see a long, narrow corridor vanishing into the darkness, brick-lined on one side. There was no floor and so he hopped from rafter to rafter as he heard his enemies squeezing into the space behind him.

His plan was to find the door to an attic in one of the neighboring houses and then descend, terrifying the house's occupants and a maid or two if need be, to street level and then be out and away. He flung open the first door he came to and stepped into a cluttered box room filled with a child's toys, luggage cases, a dress-maker's mannequin and other paraphernalia. He made for the door and cursed when he found it locked. He could hear the approach of his pursuers down the passageway and looked around desperately.

He saw the window and was up at the latch in a flash, heaving up the sash. He managed to squirm through the aperture just as the first of the men entered the box room. The rain hammered down on him, and the slate tiles were slippery. Several came loose and clattered down to the street below as he scrambled along the roof.

The terrace ended in a gabled house, with a small balcony above a larger one. The drop was still too far, but there was a small gatehouse to St. Georges Gardens just over the mews that had a sloping roof and a little chimney. Lazarus dropped down onto the first balcony, grabbing at its iron railings. The Siamese men were scurrying along the roof much more nimbly than he had managed, not loosening any tiles. He dropped down to the balcony below and climbed up onto its railing.

Lazarus leapt through the rain and landed heavily on the slanted roof of the gatehouse, loosening an avalanche of slates. He slid down with them, landing on all fours on the gravel path that led into the gardens. He looked up. His pursuers were contemplating the balconies and the leap. Men and women walked up and down the street, huddled under umbrellas. He snatched one from the nearest gentleman.

"I say!" the man cried. "You! Thief!"

Lazarus ignored him and hurried down the street to mingle with as many people as he could see. The pavement was a sea of black umbrellas, and he knew that if his pursuers had reached street level yet they hadn't a hope in Hell of picking him out of the crowd.

He continued walking to Brunswick Square and then hailed a cab. He shook off his stolen umbrella and got in. He felt around in his jacket pocket for the bundle of papers he had taken from the journal. They had not got wet, and he quickly glanced at them. It had taken a mere moment to swap the journal pages with whatever notes and documents he could gather from the desktop, and he had only finished cramming them into the leather book and retying the string before Westcott had come into the study. He smiled when he thought of Westcott's rage when he discovered that his precious journal contained his own notes and not the pages so valued by the both of them.

"Where to, guv?" the cab driver asked.

"Edmonton," Lazarus replied. "I'll give you the address when we're near it."

He was bruised and bleeding, but he had the journal at last and there was only one person on earth that he wanted to share his company with right now.

Chapter Six

In which our hero learns his true name

The house in Edmonton was a grotty little two-bedroom place of red brick, with a bay window that had not been washed in years. Lazarus took a key from his pocket and let himself in. It was dark inside and a single gas lamp burned in the back room. He entered and removed his cap. The old man on the couch, blankets mounded on top of him, turned and gave him a flicker of a smile.

"Hello, son."

"Hello, sir," Lazarus replied.

"You look like you've been in the wars."

"When am I ever not?"

The man did not reply nor smile at the jest. Lazarus sat down and looked around the room. This was not the house he had spent much of his childhood in. That had been a fine place in Pentonville. His guardian and the closest thing he ever had to a father had been forced to move to more humble dwellings before Lazarus had reached the age of fifteen. The small pile of cherished leather-bound tomes in the corner was all that remained of the vast library he had whiled away many hours of his youth in, reading about Ancient Egypt, the Punic Wars, the Gupta Empire and fabled Babylon.

And the snow-haired old man, feeble with disease

on the couch before him, was all that was left of the upright explorer who had plucked him from the slums of Bangkok and brought him back to London to raise as his own.

"How are you?" Lazarus asked the man, trying to keep the pity from his voice, refusing to believe that this strong man who had been his mentor and father figure for so many years was dying.

"Doc was here earlier, blasted quack," said Alfred Longman, explorer, abolitionist and Fellow of the Royal Geographical Society. "He bled me and is making me drink powdered nitrate with camphor water and laudanum."

"Just do what he says," Lazarus urged. "It's for the best."

Alfred doubled over in a wracking cough that lasted nearly ten seconds and brought the sweat out on his brow. "Gah! Confound this thing!" He wheezed down lungfuls of air. "Now, my boy, tell me what you've been up to and why you look like you've been engaging in bare-knuckle fisticuffs down at the docks."

"I have the journal, sir," Lazarus said. He reached into his pocket and showed his guardian the handful of papers.

Alfred's face grew even paler and he swallowed as if preparing himself. "Finally you have it. Are you sure it's the one?"

"The journal of Thomas Spencer Tyndall," Lazarus confirmed. "The very man you believe was my father."

"No doubt about it, my boy. When I caught you trying to lift my timepiece in that back alley in Bangkok, the only white street urchin in the whole city, I knew that you were something special." His lips parted in a smile of fondness at the memory. "You were such a scrawny thing but you put up such a fight when I accosted you! The other street boys had been teaching you how to fight Siamese style."

Lazarus smiled. "I wish I had been a better student. I wouldn't have so many lumps to show for myself today."

"I couldn't understand how a white boy, surely of European extraction, could have wound up living in doorways and eating toasted gutter rats," Alfred continued, his eyes misted over with reminiscence. "I did all the research I could, consulted every known traveler in those parts and all I could dig up was the name Tyndall."

Lazarus knew the story well, for it was all he had to cling to of his former life. Thomas Tyndall had been an English botanist who had moved to Bangkok with his wife and young child to study the flora of Siam. He had vanished on some trip into the hills, and his wife had died soon after. Of the child, nothing further was known. Alfred Longman was convinced that this child was the bare-footed urchin he had found living the life of a tough little pickpocket. He had rescued this boy from poverty and crime and renamed him Lazarus in honor of the saint who had been brought back from the dead.

"The journal had been purchased by a wealthy fellow in Bloomsbury," Lazarus said. "Your man Walters was a rather unscrupulous dealer. He knew I wanted the journal, and yet he sold it only days before our appointment."

"Walters is a degenerate gambler," said Alfred with distaste. "His debts have consumed his family's wealth, and that house on Cavendish Square is a ruin of its former glory." He then sighed. "Much like my own turn of fortunes. Our academic pursuits are not the only thing we have in common, it seems. But how did you get the journal from this man in Bloomsbury? I hope you didn't ruin yourself."

"The bruises you see on my face are all I let them have of me," said Lazarus. "I was caught red handed in the man's study and his Siamese thugs gave me a thorough going over."

"Siamese thugs?" Alfred asked.

"But I had switched the papers before I was caught and made off with the real goods," Lazarus added with a grin.

Alfred frowned with disapproval. "You take too many chances, my boy. You always have. Your pursuit of 'adventure'—or what others would call outright danger—has always stood in the way of you becoming a serious scholar."

The grin vanished from Lazarus's face. His impetuousness had always been a point of contention between the two of them. Alfred was the typical bookish type who saw the act of travel and physical application of archaeology as a necessary evil, while Lazarus, although bookish too in his own way, had always thirsted to see the places he had read about, to feel the history etched in the weathered stones of far off lands. To him the pursuit of the academic was useless unless one actually stood in the shadow of the pyramids or smelled the festering jungle of the Yucatan.

Alfred had nearly cut him off when he had decided to enlist in the army and go to fight in the Ashanti Campaign. The aging archaeologist disapproved of imperialism and conquest with a passion and although Lazarus was far from in agreement with these things too, he needed to leave England and find his way in the world. Capital was a problem for them in those days, as it had been ever since. Their Pentonville home was long gone, along with any chance of further education for Lazarus. The only way he could escape the life of a clerk or a librarian in London and see the world for himself was to enlist and take his chances in the African wars.

"I might be inclined to agree with you this time, sir," Lazarus told his guardian. "This fellow is a serious piece of work. He tried to have me killed in a house in Stepney. He lured me there by leaving his calling card with Walters. He's surrounded himself with nimble fighters from Siam that I don't stand a chance against. I only escaped by outwitting one, and nearly met my end at his Bloomsbury residence. He wants me dead, and doubly so since I escaped with his journal. I have no doubt that he will try again."

"Then you must keep yourself hidden from him," said Alfred. "Your clothes, they are a disguise?"

"Alas no, but they may function as one. I am working for the government again."

Alfred closed his eyes and squeezed them tight as if in pain. "I cannot have this argument with you again, son. You must do as you see fit but it breaks my heart that you sell yourself so cheaply. What business do they have you on this time?"

"There's some trouble brewing in the East End. It's to do with Bismarck's visit. Some worries about the Jews and the Socialists. I really shouldn't be discussing it with you."

"Then don't. I have no wish to hear of our government's war against the working class. Bismarck is a bloody-handed tyrant. He speaks of peace, but how many Poles and Jews have suffered at his hands? He's no better than the Kaiser he serves."

"I won't be drawn into a political debate with you, sir," said Lazarus. "For we both know that our views are the same and argument is pointless. But I have my living to make."

"A living you choose to make as the bulldog of Whitehall rather than through the study of the past."

"It pays better," said Lazarus. He felt bitter now. Of all the suffering he had felt in life, the disapproval of this man he had never even been able to call 'father' stung the most. "I want to get you into a good hospital. You've been sick these three years past. It can't go on."

"I won't be coddled by you, boy. You go and make your living. I tried to make mine through honest pursuits and you can see how that has served me in my old age."

"I will help you, sir. I will somehow pull together the capital to have you moved into Guy's."

"Just worry about yourself. You've got enough to deal with without thinking of me. Beware this man you tangle with. He sounds most dangerous. Do you know his name?"

"Yes, he introduced himself as Constantine Westcott."

Alfred sucked the air in between pursed lips as if in terrible agony. This brought about another fit of coughing which Lazarus tried to relieve by fetching him a glass of water. Alfred sipped some, but most ran down his chin, which Lazarus mopped up with the corner of his blanket.

"Son," Alfred began when he was able to speak once more, "you must forgive me. What I am about to tell you I do so out of necessity but it is a secret I had hoped to keep from you. I only hid the truth out of fear that it would harm you. Now I see that it still has the power to bring you pain these many years later, and for that I am sorry." His eyes rolled sadly in their sunken sockets and focused on Lazarus. "Constantine Westcott is your cousin."

Lazarus felt a great sinking pit in his stomach. "Cousin? Then I have family here? In London? Family that you knew of!"

"Forget them! They are bad eggs, the lot of them! When I took you into my care, I sought out your relatives here in England. Tyndall had a brother who had died years previously, and no other known family. But his wife—your mother—had a brother by the name of Barnaby Westcott. I contacted him and explained who you were. I was frightened of losing you to your family, but contact him I did for I felt it was only right. My fears were in vain, for he was a proud man, uninterested in anybody but himself. He balked at the thought of being lumbered with a half-feral nephew who had been presumed dead for several years.

"There I thought the matter closed. But a little after your fourteenth birthday, Westcott contacted me. He had somehow reversed his previous attitude and now wanted custody of you. I was more than a little surprised and so I did some asking around. Those who knew Barnaby Westcott said that he hadn't the slightest interest in raising a nephew, but was more concerned with your father's inheritance that might be due him should he take charge of you. I tried to find out what this inheritance was, but in vain. He took me to court. It was a long, hard battle, but I won in the end and Westcott had to leave you be."

"And all this happened when I was fourteen?" Lazarus asked. "Just before you had to sell up Pentonville? The court costs..."

"Bankrupted me, yes."

"Sir, I..."

"You have no cause to feel any guilt in this matter, my boy. I would have done it a hundred times over to keep you in my charge. Besides, once I knew that Westcott wanted you for nefarious purposes, I knew that I had to conceal you to keep you safe. So I sold up and moved here, telling nobody. For a few years it appeared to have worked, even though we lived in biting poverty. And now it seems that Barnaby's son has found you at last."

"But I don't understand," Lazarus said. "Why does Constantine want me dead? That would suggest that there is some truth to all that inheritance rot."

"Perhaps there is. As I said, I never could find anything out. Your father vanished without a trace and your mother died of her grief in their tenement in Bangkok. But, lord son, here we sit pondering the answers when you have your father's very journal in your hands! Let us have a look!"

Lazarus examined the bundle of papers he held. There appeared to be a good deal missing, for the first entry began rather abruptly, but he began to read it aloud.

November 16th, 1863,

We have made our passage into the Phetchabun Mountains, and as I write this we sit amidst these ramparts that fence the Khorat

Plateau off from the rest of Siam. Tomorrow we shall begin our descent onto the plateau where, if my guide is correct, I shall find fields of the Siam tulip (Cucuma alismatifolia) and possibly hybridizations of it. Singular to northern Siam and Laos, acquisition of specimens is a must for the Botanical Garden in Calcutta and Kew back home.

The Khorat Plateau (known as the Isan region) is divided by the Phu Phan mountain range into the northern Sakhon Nakhon and the southern Khorat Basin. It is towards the northern extremities of these table-top mountains that we are headed. I still have not drawn from Kasemchai the nature of the people with whom he trades nor the location that is his destination. He has remained as secretive of his business since we first met in Ayutthaya and whenever I press him on the matter he just grins at me with those hideous teeth of his blackened by the constant chewing of the betel leaf and areca nut and shakes his head. But I draw a certain honour from his cagey attitude, for if his business is so dear to him that he must speak of it to no one, then it is a privilege indeed that I am allowed to accompany him on his journey. And so the pounds of salt wait patiently in the saddlebags of our elephant as I must wait, ever patient to discover our final destination.

I have not written of our dear elephant yet and I feel that I must allow him a little space in my journal for his is such a stout old comrade that I have come to consider him the third member of our expedition. The elephant manages about three miles an hour which is a lumbering pace indeed, but the roads are so appalling here that such a beast is invaluable. The ancient highways of the Khmer Empire are cracked and overgrown and other roads are muddy and hopelessly intraversable. But the elephant keeps us high above the dust on the former and out of the mud on the latter. And in the steep climbs of the mountains he hauls himself up with the use of his trunk, grasping at firm boulders as we might stretch out a hand in a scramble.

The leeches are a constant nuisance and I am forced to smear lime on any exposed skin to ward them off. One can smell the bad air here, even in the mountains which are not high enough to afford a clean lungful. I miss the cooling sea breeze of the coast and am forever fearful of sickness. I dose myself with quinine to avoid jungle fever and drink only tea—never cold water—to avoid cholera. The border of Laos lies not far away where Henri Mouhot—the Frenchman I met in Bangkok some years ago—died raving from a fever in some squalid village, and I am terribly afraid that I too might never return from my journey. Should I fall to the same sickness, there are no good doctors nor western medicine up here in these mountains and I would die the death of many an explorer, burning up and deluded, never to return to Bangkok and see my Sarah or little Michael again.

As I sit here looking down onto the plain below, it feels like I am on the edge of one world peering down into another which lies dark and shrouded, filled with unknown dangers and delights. But such is the lot of the explorer; to delve into the unknown and take both wonder and terror in equal measure.

Lazarus stopped reading. He knew he had to continue, but could not tonight. It was late and he was dog tired. Besides, the entry he had just read presented enough information for him to digest for one night. He looked up at Alfred, his mentor, his guardian, but never his father.

"Well, my boy," Alfred said with a smile that was not untouched by sadness. "You have found your true name at last."

Lazarus looked down at the cracked leather of the journal's cover. He knew his name; the name his real mother and father had given him.

Michael.

Chapter Seven

In which two friends are found in unlikely circumstances

"Now then, lads," said Tappy, "Form a line and when I calls you forward, empty out your pockets and knapsacks onto the table. I don't want to hear any complaints. If you ain't a thief then you ain't got nothing to hide. Lively, now!"

There was a good deal of grumbling as the entire workforce lined up before the table where the manager sat, looking like a bulldog chewing a wasp. An announcement had just been made concerning a certain number of tools that had been pilfered from the workshop. Everybody was a suspect and this spot check at the end of their shift would cost them all time from their homes and families.

Lazarus sidled up behind old Kovalev. There was much peering over shoulders as each man emptied out his coat and trousers and plonked his meager belongings down for inspection. Kovalev's turn came and he dutifully showed the manager that he was not the thief. As he was putting away his things Lazarus stepped up and took out his battered old pocket watch, his penknife, his tobacco tin, a pencil, a small comb and his copy of the Commonweal.

The manager instantly saw this last item and picked it up with a sneer which he then extended to Lazarus.

He tossed the publication back down on the table. "Off with you, leftist," he said.

Lazarus caught Kovalev eyeing the paper as he stuffed it back into his jacket pocket. "Just some light reading somebody recommended," Lazarus told him.

Kovalev's only reply was a slow nod.

The identity of the thief was never revealed, but items stopped disappearing from the workshop. The following day Kovalev approached Lazarus during one of their tea breaks. He had purposely set himself apart from the rest of the group as they smoked their cigarettes and pipes and enjoyed one of the last warm days of the year before autumn fully set in.

"So, what do our friends in the Socialist League have to say about us dockers?" the Russian said in a low voice.

"Oh, the Commonweal?" Lazarus replied. "I'm not really in with them, you know."

"Who are you in with then?"

"I haven't made up my mind yet. Just trying to hear all sides and develop an informed opinion."

"You seem remarkably wise for a dock worker, I hope you don't mind my saying. Why are you here and not in some job more suited to your education?"

"I am afraid I am something of a charlatan. I have no formal education. I grew up in Stepney and my father taught me to read and write. All else I learned on my own. I joined the military and after I got wounded in the Soudan I had to make do back home without a penny to my name."

"Much like myself," said Kovalev. "I come from Smolensk. Literate, but not highly educated. Education speaks nothing for a foreigner here anyway. I could have been a clerk or a banker in my own country. Here

I am barely trusted to carry a crate without dropping it."

"My countryman's distrust of the foreigner is despicable," Lazarus agreed.

"As are our respective countries' abandonment of the soldiers who protect the lazy bourgeoisies. To fight for one's country, only to face starvation and unemployment upon return is disgusting. And even the jobs that are available are little more than slavery. Dangerous and poorly paid. There was a boy here last month who lost his leg when it was crushed by a derrick with a faulty knot. And all he got for his agony was a dismissal. Now he is a cripple on the street. The rest of us, we brave the dangers and the long days for our fivepence an hour because we must."

"And we're the lucky ones," Lazarus said. "I pass the call-on crowd every day. Most of them would sell their mother for an hour's work."

"Aye, and the work dries up as soon as a vessel is delayed by a storm. There's no stability."

"Surely there must be some way for us to get organized," said Lazarus, "like the tailors or the gasworkers."

"Trouble is that no one union is large enough to stand up to the masters. There's a general laborers union over at Tilbury Docks led by Ben Tillett, and there's the Amalgamated Stevedore's Protection League, but if there's to be strike action then the unions have to talk to one another. But anarchists disagree with Social Democrats. Jew disagrees with fellow Jew and *goy* alike. They call themselves union-this and united-that but who is to unite all these unions?"

The whistle blew for them all to get back to work.

"Listen, you seem like a sharp fellow," said Kovalev.

"If you're really interested in all this strike talk then I can introduce you to a few fellows in a club I'm a member of."

"Really? That would be very welcoming of you."

"What about your friend?" He indicated Mr. Clumps with apprehension. The mechanical was hanging around, waiting for Lazarus to rejoin the workers. "Has he got a mind of his own?"

"Don't be fooled by him," Lazarus said. "He's a simple fellow but has a good heart and more brains than he lets on. He's kosher."

"Phossy jaw, wasn't it? That's what I heard at least. Thought that only happened to matchstick girls."

"He worked in the navy factories putting together distress flares."

"Another example of the government's disregard for the welfare of those upon whose backs they stand. He's welcome to come along as well."

The club was on Berner Street in Whitechapel, and went by 'The Working Men's Educational Society'. It was a small building, but that did not deter people from massing around its doorway that Friday afternoon in a great squeeze to find seats. Most were Jews, and the gathering of such a large number of the heathen sparked off an anti-alien outburst from somebody across the street. "Bloody Lipskis!"

Lazarus frowned and turned to Kovalev. "I've been out of London for the past few years," he said. "I'm unfamiliar with current slang."

"Just a tarred brush they paint us all with," Kovalev answered. "Israel Lipski lived over on Batty Street, just a block from here. He murdered a girl six months pregnant by pouring nitric acid down her throat. He was hanged last year. His trial was a circus and only increased the hatred of the English for London's Jews."

By the time they got into the club, there were no places left on the long benches that faced the stage. Some kind soul offered up his seat to Kovalev. Lazarus and Mr. Clumps hovered behind him until somebody complained that Mr. Clumps's massive frame was blocking their view of the stage. The mechanical lumbered off and stood by the wall.

Lazarus examined the press of people. They were well-dressed for the most part, working class certainly, but clean and respectable as if they were all wearing their Sunday best. There were nearly equal parts men and women. Some were selling copies of the *Arbeter Fraynd*; the club's Yiddish paper which meant 'Worker's Friend'. Most knew Kovalev and spoke to him in Russian, German, Yiddish and English. In fact, the number of languages being spoken in the room was astonishing.

"Are all these people members?" Lazarus asked Kovalev.

"No," the old man replied. "Most are just curious members of the public like yourselves who come along to hear the speakers. I'll introduce you to my comrades afterwards."

The main speaker was a man named Yoshka Briedis who spoke on the subject of white slavery in the city of London. He began by outlining the hardships faced by the laboring class, in particular by the immigrant who must flee pogroms and persecutions in his homeland, only to find himself a slave to the 'thieving class' here in the wealthiest city in the world. He brought to light the awful reality of the sweatshops where tailors stitched clothing for fourteen hours a day;

dulling their eyesight, clogging up their lungs with stuffy air and cloth fibers, denied even the shortest of breaks so that their targets were met. Wives must bring them tea and bread and drop it down their throats while they continued to work. He spoke of the matchgirl's strike of July, of their exposure to the terrible white phosphorus that rotted their jaws. The speaker even touched on the poor women who were so desperate that they must sell their bodies on the street and face murder at the hands of the demented individual who stalked Whitechapel by night.

"Are we living in a city with people or in a forest with wild animals?" Mr. Briedis exclaimed. "That in the very heart of so-called civilization one either starves for want of bread or is murdered in the pursuit of it! We all know the concept of private property can only lead to economic enslavement!" There was a cheer from the crowd at this, which seemed to spur Briedis on to hammer home the anarchist message. "Property is a falsehood! Everything belongs to everyone! And no society ever changed without bloodshed, for no government is willing to give up its power without a fight. The class war is not only necessary, but inevitable!"

The speaker appeared to have finished and the room broke into rapturous applause. Lazarus could see the harsh logic borne of desperation by these people even if the final result unnerved him. If there was any group of revolutionists in London that would have Whitehall's drawers in a knot, then it was these chaps.

Afterwards, they adjourned to the refreshment room where hot tea was served and the club members struck up *La Marseillaise*. They were in high spirits. Kovalev was in his element; doing the rounds of the room, shaking hands and introducing his guests. Mr. Clump's mask and tale of horrible disfigurement had them all enthralled.

"And yet, no matter how horrible the conditions are in the factories, people will still bear them for they have no other choice," said one.

"Because the lowly London worker has it worse than the Negroes in the old slavery days," said a youngish man whom they had not been introduced to. "At least their masters had to feed them to keep them working. Here people drop dead from hunger and there is always some other poor bugger willing to step into his predecessor's shoes."

"Well, I'm not defending the London masters," said Kovalev, "but I think that's an unfair comparison. Here there is no lash or branding."

"Not in the physical sense," said the young man. "But metaphorically this society lashes us all with unsafe working conditions, brands us with class definitions, and keeps us all in bondage through hunger. My name is Levitski, by the way."

Lazarus took his extended hand and introduced himself and Mr. Clumps.

"You both look to be in rather fine condition for dock workers," Levitski commented. He had a thin, mousy face and nasal tone that Lazarus did not like. "Most dockers are like Comrade Kovalev here; stooped, broken and bow-legged."

"Give them a couple of decades," Kovalev muttered bitterly, "and they won't look so different from me."

"We are both new to the trade," Lazarus explained. "Mr. Clumps was in the navy factories, as you know, and I was in the military."

"Really? A military man? Most interesting."

"But getting back to the question of feeding the country's workforce," said the other man, "have you read that article in the Evening Post? About the future of the English workforce should this country go the way of the Americas?"

"Steam cabs and all that?" said Kovalev. "Can't see it happening, myself. At least not in my lifetime. The Americans are leagues ahead of us, technologically speaking."

"Only because they struck veins of that blasted mechanite stuff," said Levitski. "Its discovery didn't spell the end for just cab horses. Do you think they would have passed that emancipation act if they still relied on slavery for their industry? The mechanite furnace rendered the Negro obsolete."

"I disagree," said Kovalev. "The United States was pushing for emancipation long before mechanite was struck. That was how the war started in the first place, although few remember it now. Who knows how things might have turned out had the mineral never been discovered? Besides, are you telling us that the replacement of human slavery with a mechanized workforce is a bad thing?"

"Not at all, but imagine what such an industrial revolution might mean for a country that has no slaves."

"Oh, England has slaves, all right," said another man. "Weren't you listening to the speech in there? You're looking at us!"

"Exactly," Levitski continued. "And what happens to us when England starts building her own mechanicals to work in her factories, to till her fields and to mine her resources? We'll all go the way of the

Negro; jobless, landless and penniless. Emancipation means nothing if there is nothing to do but starve."

"But you're forgetting one important thing," said Lazarus. Levitski blinked at him expectantly. "To build mechanicals, one needs mechanite. And both the United and Confederate States have an embargo on mechanite against all nations."

"And how long will this embargo last should the European powers start picking sides? Neutrality has gone on for nigh on thirty years but that's no insurance that Britain won't throw its support behind the Confederacy tomorrow. Then it will only be a matter of time before mechanicals will be replacing us in the factories, taking over the docks and walking shoulder to shoulder with us in the streets. I say, more tea, Comrade Clumps?"

They left the club with Kovalev. It was still early and the shadows had only just begun to lengthen. "Why did you not introduce us to Mr. Levitski earlier?" Lazarus asked their host.

"Because not all of my comrades are worth your time. Levitski is an untrustworthy fellow. He talks big but contributes little. The others put up with him, but I don't like the man."

Lazarus felt that there was more to this dislike than Kovalev was letting on, but did not press it. They bade each other good night and the old Russian headed off to his home in Mile End.

"Well, Comrade Clumps," said Lazarus. "I don't know about you, but I'm dying for a drink. All that talk of class war and economic enslavement has my ears ringing and the air in that place parches the throat."

"Do you think that any of those fellows are the dangerous men Morton is interested in?" Mr. Clumps said.

"Hard to say. I wouldn't trust any of them overly, I'll say that much, but there seems to be an awful lot of pipesmoke being blown about in that house and very little in the way of real plans. They are all eager to debate the 'inevitable class war', but then they adjourn for tea and merry renditions of French revolutionary songs. I don't think any of them are serious enough to warrant my filing a report on them with the bureau. Still, I'd like to probe a little deeper."

"Maybe you could drop some hints insinuating that you are made from sterner stuff," said Mr. Clumps. "That way you might draw out the real hardliners, if there are any."

Lazarus was genuinely surprised. "Mr. Clumps, old boy, you are learning fast. Now, let's see about that drink."

Whitechapel Road often surprised the newcomer by its apparent respectability. The pit of filth and degradation as depicted in the newspapers was largely exaggerated. It was certainly not an upmarket high street but the friendly hawkers and market stall owners, public houses, shops and gin palaces were a far cry from the Sodom or Gomorrah painted by the press.

Steam from the nearby railway hung in great white plumes above the gabled rooftops, while the tune cranked out by an organ-grinder drifted across the street. Men smoking pipes leaned in doorways and in the entrances to dim and gloomy alleyways. Children spent away their pennies in shooting galleries, and some stood in awestruck fascination as a foreigner did tricks with a white rat. A variety of colorful characters shouted out the benefits of whatever they were selling; new and improved boot-polish, curiously strong mints and pamphlets of poetry for only 3d. In the window of a Jewish shop, Lazarus saw books in Hebrew amidst various objects pertaining to synagogue worship. Even at the tail end of the day the whole street was alive with the multi-layered colors of life.

But underneath this façade of noise and bustle, the reminders of what had occurred in those black passages beyond the shop fronts in the darkest hours of the night were ever present. A fat man with a waxed moustache drew in customers to a ghoulish waxworks show depicting the recent killings in as much gory detail as possible. A notice in a shop window offered a reward of a hundred pounds for the apprehension of the perpetrator. A newspaper boy wandered past waving a folded paper that promised more on the brutal monster that stalked the shadows of the night.

As they stepped off the high street into one of the alleys, Lazarus immediately felt as if they had trespassed into another world. It was instantly darker and colder. The tall, shabby buildings loomed over the narrow cobbles, blocking the sunlight. The sounds were different here; an old woman's pneumonic coughing, a baby screaming and the raised voices of a man and a woman engaged in an argument. The stiff corpse of a cat festered a few feet away. Here was the real beating heart of Whitechapel; the rotten core of London's East End, hidden from the bustle of the shops and stalls, a world where human suffering rippled down its streets and washed over one like a tide of black misery and despair.

As they passed the warehouses that overshadowed Buck's Row—the small alleyway where Polly Nichols had met her fate—Lazarus could see in through grimy street level windows and down into dim basements, where the sweaters were hard at work sorting old clothes, cobbling boots and making shirts. It was oddly quiet here but for a dog barking.

The light had begun to fade and already several prostitutes were about their business, walking in twos or threes, shabby-looking and worn down. As they passed the entrance to another winding alleyway, they heard a muffled groan of protest. Something about the noise struck Lazarus as altogether different from the many sounds of woe and misery that echoed down those grim streets. This was a desperate sound escaping from a mouth that had been abruptly stifled.

They peered down the alley, and in the dim light they could make out the form of a woman being pressed against the wall by a heavy-set man in a bowler hat.

"Stay close to me," Lazarus told Mr. Clumps, "but let me handle this."

At their approach, the man turned to glare at Lazarus with mean eyes set in an unshaven face. One meaty fist held a prostitute in a bright red dress against the wall, his fingers digging in deep to choke off her breathing. His other hand held a short folding knife.

"You ain't no copper," he remarked. "So piss off, or I'll give you worse'n what I'm about to give her!" Then his eyes widened as he noticed Mr. Clumps shuffling out of the gloom. "Christ!" He stood back and changed his grip on the knife as if he might thrust it out in a gutting motion.

Lazarus drew his Bulldog pocket revolver and aimed it as his ugly forehead. "Try it and see what you get," he said.

The thug grinned, folded up his knife and put it into his breast pocket, removing a similar revolver with the same hand. He was either mad or extremely careless with his life, for Lazarus could see in his eyes that the man intended to shoot. Apparently so did Mr. Clumps for, in a burst of speed that Lazarus would not have thought the mechanical capable of, he was between the thug and Lazarus, his massive chest blocking the gun's muzzle.

The shot went off and the girl screamed. Mr. Clumps did not even flinch. Lazarus knew that the shot had not damaged him; as with all mechanicals there was a screen of iron plating that protected the organic pilot's innards. But the thug was none the wiser.

"Wha... what the bloody hell are you?" the man stammered through the gunsmoke, his eyes wide. He did not have time to chamber another round for Mr. Clumps's massive fist crashed into his jaw, sending him sliding across the cobbles and into the filth.

"That wasn't too savage, I hope?" Lazarus said.

"Not too savage," the mechanical replied, flexing his gloved hand.

The thug groaned and rolled onto all fours, his hand reaching up to his bloodied mouth. A tooth fell loose. Lazarus aimed a kick at his backside.

"Be off with you before we decide to rid the streets of you permanently!"

The thug staggered to his feet and vanished into the dark warren. Lazarus looked at the woman, and for the first time realized how young she was. Perhaps in her early twenties, dressed in a Lindsey frock with a clean white apron. She had a mass of strawberry-blonde curls that spilled down on either side of her slender neck. Compared to the ruddy-faced, rotten-toothed women who shared her profession, this one shone with a youthful exuberance yet unspoiled by the ravages of her trade. And she was beautiful.

"Much obliged sirs," she said, rearranging her curls, but not taking her wary eyes off Mr. Clumps.

"What was he about?" Lazarus asked, putting away his pistol.

"One of the High-Rips," she replied. "Thinks he owns me and my services."

"The High-Rips?"

"A gang. They take money from girls like me every week and if we can't pay 'em then they take something else instead."

"I see," said Lazarus.

"You fellas ain't from around here, are you?" she said, studying them.

"No, we, ah, live in Limehouse and are just here for a meeting with friends."

"Well if you're looking for a good time, my name's Mary and I'd be happy to oblige. If I don't take your fancy, then I have a friend who…"

"That won't be necessary," said Lazarus.

She eyed him warily. "Are you a copper?"

"No."

"You talk fine but your clothes say you're a laborer. I thought you might be down here looking for that murderer."

"No, as I said, we were at a meeting with some friends."

"Well, I'm very glad you were passing, I'll say that. Would you mind accompanying me a little further? A girl can't get enough protection these days. I'll buy you both a drink."

"That would be very nice."

"The night hasn't started yet, and I always need a glass of gin to get me going. The *Ten Bells* isn't far. I usually go there of a night. Is your friend all right?" She eyed the smoking hole in Mr. Clumps's shirt.

"Him? Oh, yes. Very strong constitution. Built like an ox."

"I know someone as can stitch him up if he needs it."

"Do you require medical attention?" Lazarus asked his companion.

"No," said Mr. Clumps. "Barely scratched me. I've stopped bleeding already."

"All these coppers and vigilance committees after this bloody murderer," the girl muttered as they walked on. "They need look no further than the Hoxton High-Rips. If anyone's murderin' us street girls then it's them."

"You really think a gang is responsible for the killings?" Lazarus asked.

"S'gotta be. Those lot are animals. Old Martha Tabram, they said, owed them just half a crown and they stabbed her thirty-nine times, the papers said. And you just pointed a gun at one of them. Should've shot him."

"Perhaps I should have."

"They only get worse. Stabbing a girl thirty-nine times is one thing but now they've started taking organs. Some say it's to sell to medical students but we know a message when we sees one. They want us to be afraid. They want us to think that we're to be next to lose our guts."

"Were no organs taken from Martha Tabram at all?" Lazarus asked her.

"Nope. The coppers reckon that means it wasn't the same man who done the other two, but I dunno. What's to stop them raising their game with each knifing? Getting a taste for it, as it were."

Lazarus didn't answer. The police's opinions about the first victim were troubling. If Martha Tabram had been killed by a different man, then perhaps it wasn't so heartening that Mansfield had not woken up in the lime oast following her murder.

The *Ten Bells* on the corner of Commercial Road and Fornier Street seemed to be a regular haunt of Mary's. She was recognized by several street girls and men alike who called out greetings to her which she heartily returned. It was already busy when they got there, and an elderly woman was selling roasted chestnuts by the door. They went in and found a dark booth. Lazarus refused Mary's money and bought them all large glasses of gin.

"Am I right in saying there's a little Irish in you?" he asked her as she knocked back half of the stinging liquid.

She smiled at him with big blue eyes. "Right you are. I was born in Limerick, but we left when I was still a little girl."

"And that's when you came to London?"

She knocked back the rest of her gin, wincing a little as she swallowed, shaking her head. "No. My da took us to Wales. He was an ironworker. Me, my mam and my six brothers and sister lived in a shabby little cottage in Caernarvonshire. Buy me another drink and I might teach you some Welsh."

Lazarus laughed and drained his own glass. He went back to the bar and returned with another round. Mr. Clumps dutifully emptied his second one more or less instantly and Lazarus began to wonder if he would indeed see a drunk mechanical before the evening was out.

It was not long before Lazarus and Mary were both rosy-cheeked and laughing loudly. It had grown late and the street outside was dark. The public house was heaving with people. Lazarus was amused by Mary's stories about her time in Wales. Her eyes shone with a brilliant energy, and he found it hard to believe that she was the same breed as those sad, broken women he had seen in Whitechapel earlier that day, destroyed by drink and consumed by the hideous and violent world in which they lived.

"What made you come to London?" he asked.

At this, her face lost its glow and her brilliant eyes dulled to a melancholy grey. "I fell in love with a collier. I was only sixteen and my mam and da didn't approve of him so we ran off together and got married on the sly. He died in a mine explosion two years later. I couldn't go back home, so I moved to Cardiff where I lived with my cousin for a while and then on to London."

"Do you miss your people?"

At this her face grew angry. "No. They hate me and what I am and I don't need 'em. I don't want no one's pity neither!" she said, catching his expression. "I haven't always been an East End bag-tail you know. I used to work in a fancy place in the West End where all the French girls work. Only toffs bought my services there. None of the tuppenny fuck-hunters you get round here. And I can read and write too, I've got a good education."

She was drunk and fiery and Lazarus was thrilled by her. She was so full of energy, so full of spirit to fight back against the world that threatened to destroy her.

"I'm an artist too, you know that? A good one. This game is just to tide me over 'til I can make enough money from my drawings so's I don't have to live on my back no more. And that won't be too long. One of them gypsies in Spitalfields Market read my palm. She said that my life will change in a matter of weeks. I'm just waiting for the right bit of luck to come along. Have you ever been to Spitalfields Market?"

"Not recently."

"They've got everything there. There's this hypnotist woman who can make a person believe anything. I saw her convince a man that he was a monkey. You should have seen him hopping about the place and scratching his arse! The power of the mind is a hundred times stronger than the body, the hypnotist said. And the funny thing was, when the man snapped out of it he had no memory of his a-capering about!"

They laughed at this and then talked some more, but after a while, Mary gave him the soberest look she could muster and informed him that she had to leave.

"It's been nice talking to you mister, and thank you for everything, your friend too, but I need to start earning my money. With nothing to pay off them High-Rips, I'll be for it and no mistake."

Lazarus felt reluctant to let her go, especially as he knew the dangerous game which she would be playing that night. He wanted to give her money so she wouldn't have to, but knew she would refuse. She wanted no one's pity and no one's charity. She had to fight the world on her own terms. She stood up to go, and leaned over to kiss him lightly upon his cheek.

"If you ever want me, you know where to find me now," she said.

"Mary who?" he asked her. "So I know who to ask for."

"Kelly. Mary Jane Kelly." And then she was gone,

clutching her shawl about her shoulders as she sauntered of into the crowded Whitechapel night.

Chapter Eight

In which the killer strikes again

November 17th, 1863

If this is the 'cool' season, then I have no wish to experience Siam's 'hot' season here on the plains of Khorat. The sun is not so much blistering, but it pulses its heat from behind a screen of clouds and causes all around to fester in a humid hum of sweltering stickiness. The monsoon season ended in October and the rivers are still swollen with runoff from the mountains. We must surely be back in Bangkok by February as the hot season will be unbearable.

The rivers here are choppy and fast and it is rare to see any boats at all much less the swarms of narrow, covered canoes that carry their cargoes of indigo, teak, fish, rice and vegetables further south. But the landscape is so abundant in fruits and produce that one has to wonder what happens to it all, for there are few people about to harvest the profits. Mangrove, betel and tamarind are in abundance, as are the thick clusters of bamboo and sugar cane and with no scythe to cut them down they must surely rot away wastefully.

There is also a notable abundance of the Siamese Rosewood (Dalbergia cochinchinensis) known to the natives as 'Phayung'. In the flatter plains further south, the cotton bush grows thick during the hot season and makes the region (if not the entire country) an exciting prospect to my countrymen. The hostilities on the American continent are a constant worry to Britain and

France who rely so much on the cotton plantations of those southern states blockaded by the Union. Countries such as Siam, Cambodia and Egypt offer alternative sources, if only more well thought out trade agreements could be reached, or even protectorates established. But King Mongkut holds independence above all things despite his enthusiasm for the modernisation and even westernization of his own country. His push for a more civilized Siam is not at the expense of tradition, however, and it is a rare paradox to see at his court a harem of slave girls taught etiquette by the English governess he has employed to tutor his innumerable children.

We push on towards the northern tip of the Phu Phan range, our elephant bearing us along proudly, swatting at the incessant clouds of mosquitoes with bundles of foliage he plucks up from the surroundings for the job. I have to admire the...

<pages of the journal missing>

...again. We are camped in what seems to be the thickest part of the forests that crawl up the mountains like carpets of the richest variety. I have to feel that we are nearing our destination and soon we shall turn our long suffering elephant around and return for the coast. I am more than satisfied with the fruits of our trip. My specimen boxes are overflowing and I am somewhat daunted by the task I have ahead of me in illustrating, cataloguing and dispatching my finds. All that remains of our trip is for Kasemchai to complete the business transaction with his mysterious mountain dwellers.

He has left me at our little camp, writing by the light of the fire, to meet with his people at some undisclosed location further in the forest. I have been forbidden from following. He does not even want me to see the faces of whom he sells his salt to. I, of course respect his wishes but I am more than a little unnerved at being left totally alone in the depths of the forest with darkness all around me, especially in the light of what we saw today.

Kasemchai, eyes always keen, spotted the tracks from the shoulders of our elephant and jumped down at once to inspect them. I must confess I saw nothing remarkable in the churned up mud at the foot of a fallen trunk but in these dark churnings, like a gypsy lady peering at tea leaves, he saw the spoor of some large predator.

"Tiger," he told me with no ambiguity of the gravity of our situation.

They are not rare in this part of the country, those striped princes of the jungle, but I have no wish to see one up close. I am told that fire keeps them away and so I have built up our campfire as high as I dare. We have no rifle with us for we are not hunters, and perhaps it was a little foolish to leave Bangkok with no thought for self-preservation from the beasts that stalk by night. I have remembered the native technique for hunting and killing the tiger, and have procured myself a stout length of bamboo which I have sharpened into a javelin with my knife. I don't know if I would have the gall or strength in my arms to do what I must if I am come upon in the night, but it is a small comfort at least to have a weapon of some primitive sort by my side as I lay down to sleep.

It is that pursuit to which I shall apply myself now, blanket over me and spear by my side as I listen to the jungle noises and await the return of my trusted guide; a return that I confess cannot come at all prematurely.

Lazarus was amazed by the diligence of the Berner Street crowd in the upkeep of their club and the distribution of its literature. For a people who constantly complained of not enough work, or long hours and low pay when there was work, they certainly gave enough time and coin towards the spreading of the anarchist message. The club refused to make a profit on principal, yet hard-earned coin rolled in. Lazarus learned that most of it came from little wooden boxes nailed to the walls in factories and sweatshops where workers would drop a penny in whenever they could spare one.

The club on Berner Street came to be their second home for a while. Meetings were held twice a week and speeches every Friday night. The rest of the time was given over to socializing, poetry recitals and the occasional play extolling the socialist ideal. No alcohol was consumed in the club but the members burned the midnight oil on tea, cake and livid discussions on politics, oppression and anarchy. It would carry on well into the early hours, when they might fall asleep on some cushions for a few hours before rising and heading off to their respective jobs.

Lazarus tried to make himself useful as best he could. When he learned that the *Arbeter Fraynd* was printed on premises in a little stables in the yard adjoining the club, he offered his services as a typesetter. Rather than sticking to a regular schedule, the 'Worker's Friend' went out whenever they could manage it and it was always a rush job. Although he didn't speak Yiddish, Lazarus could put the cast metal sorts in the correct order. He found his services greatly appreciated, as nobody seemed able to commit for more than a few days at a time due to the up and down nature of their other employments.

Levitski interested Lazarus more than any of the others. He was not altogether popular and had the reputation of a lurker; a man who would idly attend meetings without offering much but the occasional recital of the anarchist mantras, or a rendition of something he had read in the papers seemingly for the sake of appearances.

Lazarus recognized a fellow charlatan when he saw one, but there was something strange about the young Russian. He was, for the most part, placid but his occasional outbursts had the ring of viciousness about them. Most in the club abhorred violence despite their boasts of wanting to bring down the system, but Levitski spoke openly of bloodshed, and of burning London to its foundations so that a new order might arise from its ashes. Lazarus was not the only one who felt that his words were not altogether metaphorical.

It got to a point where Levitski must have realized that Lazarus was the only person who would willingly listen to his tirades. With increasing frequency, Lazarus found himself cornered by the young radical and pelted with monologues. It was not hard to cultivate a relationship of sorts with him, and Lazarus felt that if anybody in the Berner Street club warranted his attention then it was Levitski. They spent much time in each other's company. Levitski even began turning up at their lodgings in Limehouse some mornings and they would walk to the club together.

Unlike a lot of the members, Lazarus rarely spent the night at the club, preferring to get a good night's rest back at their lodgings before the drudgery of the next day's work began. But on some nights his discussions with Levitski carried him far beyond a decent hour.

It was on one of these nights when, finally able to escape the angry little Russian, Lazarus made his way down Commercial Road towards Limehouse, lighting his pipe as he walked. He had already sent Mr. Clumps home ahead of him, explaining to the mechanical for the umpteenth time that he did not require a bodyguard to walk him home every evening. Across the heads of the crowd he suddenly spotted his friend Mansfield.

Mansfield wore a slouch hat and a black cloak as one trying to conceal his identity, but to one who knew him of old, he stuck out like a sore thumb in the crowded street. The presence of his troubled friend in Whitechapel was worrisome to say the least, in the light of Mansfield's concerns over his involvement in the murders. If he feared that he was a danger to the streetwalkers of this area then why in God's name did he risk coming down here of a night?

The writhing mass of cobbled labyrinths that made up Whitechapel still swarmed with the grotesque and decadent visions of nightlife. Lazarus pounded down Commercial Road, struggling to maintain visual contact due to the darkness and the crowds of shuffling drunks and strutting prostitutes. He lost sight of Mansfield and cursed as he reached the end of the street before turning back, convinced he had headed off down one of the dark alleys. The task of searching each filthy backstreet was a laborious one, but Lazarus couldn't suppress the horrible feeling that a woman's life might be at stake.

He was partway down Back Church Lane when he heard some commotion one street over. That was back on Berner Street. A woman screamed. Lazarus cut across Fairclough Street and headed up towards the club, where he could see a man hovering at the gateway to the very yard where he had been working as a typesetter that day. The lurking man seemed to be peering in, but it was not Mansfield.

A man's cry of "Lipski!" from within the yard, harsh and threatening, startled the observer who took a few steps backwards and then spotted Lazarus.

They gazed at each other down the gloomy street, unable to read each other's faces. The man took off at a fast trot towards Commercial Road and Lazarus jogged over to the entrance of the yard from whence the cry had come.

The yard was black as pitch and once he had passed through the wooden gates, he could barely see three steps ahead of himself. His foot bumped against something soft and heavy. He bent down to inspect it closer and found himself peering into the grotesque mask of death itself.

He guessed her to be in her forties. She had dark curly hair. Her throat had been slashed deeply and the ground was slippery with blood. He cursed himself. He had been too late to prevent this.

There was a noise; the sound of shuffling feet on the other side of the yard. He peered into the gloom, fully aware that the killer was still near. He drew his revolver and ventured into the shadows.

"Mansfield?" he hissed, not wanting to use his friend's name too loudly lest anybody hear it. "It's me, Lazarus. It's all right, I'm here to help you."

There was no reply. He stuck to the wall and crept around. A flicker of movement caught his eye, and as he squinted he could make out a dark figure stand upright. They peered at each other through the black abyss for a while, neither moving.

The sound of a horse and cart drew near, and the small patch of light at the entrance to the yard was filled with the shadow of a man in a black coat and hat. He was mumbling some words of encouragement in

Yiddish to his horse that seemed reluctant to enter the yard. Perhaps it could smell the two men lurking in the shadows, or the blood that glistened on the cobbles.

The Jew tugged on the reigns and pulled the horse a few steps into the yard. He stopped at the exact spot Lazarus had stood and seemed to notice something on the ground. He lit a match and Lazarus immediately recognized him as Louis Diemschutz; the club's steward who regularly kept his goods in the yard's stables. As Diemschutz bent down to inspect what he had found, Lazarus realized with unease how visible he had been to Mansfield when he had entered the yard. Diemschutz had found the body, and quickly led his horse out of the yard, muttering prayers under his breath.

Lazarus turned back to the figure of his friend, but he had gone. He had clearly taken advantage of the distraction and had fled through the narrow exit from the yard between the stables. Lazarus quietly left the yard in as much haste as subtlety would allow. He had no desire to be found at the site of a new Whitechapel killing, and Diemschutz would already be making his discovery known to the lingering members inside the club. He had to track Mansfield down.

He was now under no illusions that his friend was not the killer. He had all but seen him commit his latest atrocity. As he headed up to Commercial Road his mind buzzed with mixed emotions of grief, anger and guilt. His friend had tried to convince him, desperately reached out for help, and Lazarus had not given it. Mansfield was clearly deranged, his mind broken by some unknown malady, but he had at least the sense to know that he was mad. Whatever Lazarus had to do to help him, he swore that he would do it.

But first, he had to confront this evil alter ego; this Mr. Hyde to Mansfield's Dr. Jekyll. And he knew where his friend was headed. He hailed a hansom and told the driver to take him to Limehouse.

The gigantic factories, warehouses and lime oasts rose up against the black sky like sinister giants in a twisted fairy-tale. The streets were silent as he paid for his cab, then made his way towards the old shell of a building that he had visited some weeks before. It had not changed in his absence and he had no difficulty in locating the small door that had admitted him upon his previous visit.

It was dark and grim inside, and there was no evidence that Mansfield had returned. The cab had made good time and Mansfield would still be making his way there on foot. Lazarus exited the building and found a suitable hiding place behind some shattered crates where he could lay in wait for his friend.

As he sat there, shivering with the bitter cold, questions flooded his mind that he could not find the answers to. Why did Mansfield murder? What was the cause of his insanity? And why prostitutes? The papers asked similar questions on a daily basis and it was generally thought that prostitutes represented the easiest prey for a madman set on murder. Their lowly positions, poor familial relations and professions that required them to willingly stroll down the darkest parts of the East End with strange men set them apart as easy pickings. If this was true then, insanity or no, there seemed to be some method to Mansfield's madness.

At last the sound of footsteps could be heard approaching. Lazarus peered from his hiding place as Mansfield made his way towards the old lime oast, and noted with fearful fascination how he carried himself so differently; stooped over and scuttling, *Hyde*-like. Under his arm he carried a small package.

Lazarus waited a while after Mansfield had beetled in through the side door before following in after. What little light there was, shone into the building from its broken roof. Sticking to the shadows, he watched as Mansfield approached the edge of the dock and began to unravel the sinister package. He was too far away to see its contents in any detail, but Mansfield removed what looked like several pieces of meat, still dripping. These he cast into the scum-coated water, with loud splashes.

He stood awhile, staring down at the spreading ripples, mesmerized by their movement. Was this some sort of ghastly ritual? Lazarus had no doubt about the nature of the offerings. One of the previous victims had been relieved of part of her uterus. He had not noticed that the woman in Dutfield's Yard had been cut open, but it had been too dark to see much apart from her slashed throat. But why cast this offal into the river? What monstrous thing dwelt in those murky depths that demanded blood sacrifices?

Mansfield began to sway, as if drunk. He emitted a loud, agonized moan, a howl of grief and disgust. He staggered backwards and collapsed to the dusty floor, still as if dead. Lazarus ran to him from the shadows and cradled his friend's head in his hands. Mansfield awoke and looked at him with terror-stricken eyes.

"It's happened again, hasn't it?" he whispered.

Lazarus nodded, sharing his grief, although he was relieved to see his friend's sanity return, if only for the moment.

"Oh, God, Lazarus!" he wailed. "What happened? What did I do?"

"Let's get home," Lazarus said. "I have a place nearby." He could not let Mansfield alone now; partly for the safety of the girls of Whitechapel—*girls like Mary*—and partly for the safety of his friend.

Chapter Nine

In which some help is recruited

November 23rd, 1863

I have awoken in the strangest of places and under the strangest of circumstances. A day and two nights have passed since my last journal entry in which I expressed my fears of the tiger we had seen the spoor of.

My fears that I would not be able to sleep while such a beast prowled the surrounding forest, with only my bamboo spear for protection were unfounded for I had apparently drifted off into a comfortable slumber. I have no idea at what time I awoke, only that I had been dreaming of a screaming child. Thoughts of little Michael were on my mind as I came to but I soon realised that the screams were that of a trumpeting elephant in some distress.

I seized my spear and, once again lamenting my lack of a hunting rifle or even a revolver, set off through the trees towards the ruckus. I had no light to guide me but the sounds of the animal and accompanying human cries of alarm were as a beacon to me in the darkness. I was under no doubt that the elephant was our own dear friend, and the human cries came from Kasemchai and his mysterious acquaintances.

I came to a clearing lit by burning torches. Several figures were illuminated and they had their backs to me. They were light on their feet as if anticipating some danger. Kasemchai was there and the others, who numbered five or six, wore native garments of dyed cloth and had bare chests. Then I saw the danger that had them all so panicked. There, in the centre of the clearing was a tiger. It crouched low, tail flicking back and forth, its snarling head hissing up at the nearest man, who took several hasty steps back. None of the men appeared to be armed and were doing their best not to make any sudden movements.

As I lie in my bed now, fearfully wounded, I cannot for the life of me explain my behaviour, only that it was borne out of fear for my own life as well as that of Kasemchai and these fellows I had never met. I was the only man present with a weapon that stood a chance against the cat, and so I hurried forward and put myself between the retreating man and the beast, holding my weapon low, pointed at the face of the predator.

The tiger seemed to take great offence at this and chose that moment to pounce. There was a cry of alarm from all around as the great cat leapt towards me. I stood transfixed with terror, my arms as rigid as the spear they held. The tiger landed on its point, which sank deep into its white breast, bringing forth crimson to soak the fur. It yeowled in rage and slid closer, swiping at me with its massive paw.

Had my spear not held it at a relatively safe distance I would not be alive to write this tale down. But the blow at the animal's farthest reach was a glancing one only that caught my left shoulder and part of my chest, ripping thick lines through my flesh almost to the bone.

The agony was intense and blotted out much of what followed. I do not remember hitting the ground, only a frantic terror that the beast might not be dead and still had another swipe left in its powerful limbs. I remember snatches of native language which was unintelligible to me, and of being carried somewhere. Then nothing.

This room in which I have awoken is a curious one. It is of stone but richly decorated. Wooden doors conceal the rest of the building from my eyes, but they are painted with such garish designs that they have kept me amused for many hours now. A small slit window with stone bars carved into twists lets in the jungle air but I have not had the strength to rise up and see what view I have.

The pain in my arm and chest is excruciating. I assume somebody has sewn me up, but I cannot inspect the wounds myself for they are bound tightly with cloth through which only a few spots of blood show. A strange old native man comes to check on me regularly and gives me draughts of foul tasting infusions.

Kasemchai has also been to visit and it is from him alone that I have been able to draw any sense. I killed the tiger. That he explained to me with wide eyes. He says that it was a feat that has lifted me up into the very highest esteem of the people amongst whom we now dwell. This act is only surpassed by my saving the life of a royal prince of this city who must have been the man desperately trying to edge himself out of the beast's range.

"City?" I exclaimed at the mention of the word.

"Big mountain city," Kasemchai explained with a grin. "No white man been here before. You very honoured."

That at least explains the root of his secrecy during our journey. But why should a city remain such a big secret? There are dozens of varying sizes in Siam, but even Henri Mouhot made no mention of one so far north and in such a depopulated place as Isan. I have so many questions and long to be up on my feet to seek the answers, but I fear that it will be many days before I have the strength to go exploring. Here comes my doctor again.

The Evening News
1 October 1888, Fifth Edition

THE WHITECHAPEL HORRORS. HORRIBLE MURDER OF A WOMAN NEAR COMMERCIAL ROAD.

ANOTHER WOMAN MURDERED AND MUTILATED IN ALDGATE. ONE VICTIM IDENTIFIED. BLOOD STAINED POST CARD FROM "JACK THE RIPPER." SPECIAL ACCOUNTS. A HOMICIDAL MANIAC OR HEAVEN'S SCOURGE FOR PROSTITUTION.

While Lazarus had been awaiting the arrival of his friend outside the lime oast, Mansfield had been able to kill a second woman. That would always weigh on Lazarus's conscience; that he had been hiding behind a crate while another woman was being butchered. Her name had been Catherine Eddowes, a prostitute who had met her end in Mitre Square, at the western end of Commercial Road. Her throat had been slashed, her face mutilated and her intestines pulled out. Her uterus and kidney had been removed, and only Lazarus knew that those particular items were now at the bottom of Lime-kiln Dock.

There was much discussion in the papers about the un-mutilated condition of the first victim of that night. The murder of Elizabeth Stride—a middle-aged Swedish immigrant whom misfortune had turned to prostitution—had clearly been interrupted and the papers told of two men who had come forward as witnesses; Diemschutz and the first man who had fled upon seeing Lazarus. Fortunately, neither could give much information that could be useful to the police. For now, Lazarus felt confident that he and Mansfield were safe.

The city was in an uproar. Why hadn't the police caught the killer? The fourth and fifth victims were on the mortician's slab and, the killer was taunting the police by sending letters to the press. Two had been received. The first, addressed 'Dear Boss', boasted of the previous killings and challenged the police to catch him. The second, a grubby postcard, spoke of the double murders and had many convinced that it really was penned by the killer, as it was received by Scotland Yard before the details of the recent atrocities had been publicised.

Lazarus wasn't fooled. Half the East End was savvy to the double event within hours of the police arriving on the scene, giving any pathetic thrill-seeker ample time to pen his hoax to the Yard. And the real killer was in his bedsit, under lock and key, sleeping like the very dead.

Mr. Clumps, silently loyal as ever, asked no questions when Lazarus staggered in with Mansfield draped over his shoulders in the small hours of the morning. He lay the actor down on the bed while the mechanical heated up what was left of their dinner over the fire. Mansfield was barely conscious but Lazarus forced some tea down him, along with a bit of bread and hot sausage. Then he slept, deeply, occasionally whimpering like a frightened child.

Lazarus decided that it was time he got him some help.

The *Ten Bells* was heaving with customers that evening, and the old woman selling roasted chestnuts was at the entrance again. Lazarus led the way as they waded in through the thick pipe smoke and press of bodies to the booths at the back. People parted for Mr. Clumps's massive form and Mansfield looked around nervously. Scanning the crowd for Mary, Lazarus hoped that he would not see her with a customer. There was no sign of her and so they went to the bar and ordered pints of porter.

As they stood drinking, there came the sound of a commotion on the street outside. Several customers dashed out to find the cause. Lazarus and his companions set down their drinks and joined them.

There was already a good deal of people standing on the pavement, shouting and laughing as two women fought in the street. They screamed abuse at each other and tugged each other's hair, scratching and punching each other's faces in their fury. The light curls identified one of them as Mary and she was clearly winning, egged on by the spectators who favored her. The other was a blonde woman; a little older but clearly in the same profession.

The two wildcats tumbled over onto the muddy cobbles as they pounded and pummeled each other. Mary quickly gained the upper hand, clambering atop the blonde woman. With a savage swing of her fist, she sent blood streaming from her opponent's nose. The woman cried out and let go of Mary's hair. Mary got up amidst a roaring cheer and glowered down at the beaten woman, hands on her hips, her beautiful face twisted with proud triumph. The blonde woman scrambled to her feet, clutching her bloody nose and took off down the street, aided by a hard kick to her hind quarters from Mary's boot.

The crowd roared with laughter and many shouted

their congratulations to Mary.

"You saw her off and no mistake!"

"Gave that tart a right hidin'!"

"She won't be back, Mary!"

The scene over, the crowd meandered back into The *Ten Bells* and Mary stood rubbing the mud off her skirt.

"I hope I never get on your wrong side," Lazarus said as she came towards them.

She threw him a smile. "There's too many bag-tails as it is round the *Ten Bells*. Mesself and a few of my pals, this is our patch and God help any bitch who thinks otherwise." She looked at him with her head tilted to one side, her bright blue eyes curious. "What brought you back to Whitechapel? Couldn't keep away from me, eh? And you've brought another friend." She examined Mansfield's clothes. "Quite a toff he is too."

"Um, thank you," said Mansfield not sure if he had been complimented or not.

"You are a mysterious one, Mr. Longman," she said. "I don't feel that I know what to make of you. One minute you're a docker, the next a companion for well-dressed men. One day I'll get the story from you."

"I need a favor, Mary," Lazarus said.

"Well then," she replied. "Let's go inside and have a talk. I could do with a gin, anyway."

Chapter Ten

In which the darkest depths of the human mind are plumbed

'Fat women, dwarfs, a living skeleton and a giant; enough to rival Buffalo Bill's Red Indians!' advertised the gaudy sheet of canvas above the entrance to the establishment in Spitalfields Market. One of many showcases of the novel, the bizarre and the grotesque to be found in London, people thronged there of a night to satisfy their curiosity concerning all things strange and exotic for the entrance fee of a penny. On Saturday nights, dancing Zulus performed.

Lazarus paid the young lady at the entrance for the admittance of four and they wandered into the lobby. The building had once been a furniture warehouse and had since been draped with green velvet. The scarred and dusty wooden floorboards supported a variety of extraordinary and shocking exhibits reportedly donated by the British and Foreign Medicine Institute. Pickled fetuses, children with two heads and bizarre animal hybrids floated in jars of formaldehyde. Wax models of terrible deformities and diseases were gawped at by men and women in their evening dress, squirming and blanching at each and every new monstrosity that caught their eye. They drank it up with voyeuristic relish, all to the jolly tune of the organ grinder that filtered in from outside.

In the corner of the room a penny peepshow depicted gruesome portraits of the Ripper killings, and attracted a considerable crowd of both rough locals and well-dressed people from further afield, demonstrating that bad taste truly transcends class. Lazarus and his companions did not stop to waste their attention on any of this, and Mansfield did a fine job of swallowing his unease. Instead, they made their way into the next room where the main attraction was to be held.

A bill next to the sliding doors advertised the talents of Miss Buki; 'Gypsy Mystic, Mind-controller and Hypnotist!' This was what Mary had brought them to see. Lazarus had to confess as he gazed at the garish poster with its ludicrous depiction of an exotic woman projecting what seemed to be rays of light from her forehead, he seriously questioned the worth of their visit. But Mary was convinced by the woman's talents, and Lazarus so desperately wanted to help Mansfield that he was prepared to go through with just about any old bunkum.

The room was beginning to fill up and the few chairs that encircled the stage were inadequate for the number of people who pressed in to catch a glimpse of the mystic's show. Mr. Clumps parted a way for them, and not for the first time Lazarus found himself in awe of the effect mere size could have on a crowd. Several seated men even gave up their seats for them and nervously scuttled off.

As they sat down, Lazarus picked up a tattered pamphlet that had been left on his seat by its previous occupant and examined it. It was a 'penny dreadful'; one of those cheap and lurid publications that serialized the melodramatic exploits of folk heroes and villains. It was the title that caught his attention. *Sweeny Todd the Demon Barber and the Bath of Blood; a Romance of Exciting Interest.* He thumbed through it, reading a few paragraphs. It was hardly Dickens but seemed entertaining enough.

A man emerged on stage and greeted the audience as the manager of the establishment before presenting Miss Buki herself. Lazarus set the penny dreadful to one side as a modestly attired woman sauntered onstage with quiet dignity. She was not young but might still be considered attractive with her silver hair and dark, foreign eyes. Lazarus had expected a frumpish old woman with big hair and too much jewelry, mumbling incoherently over a crystal ball as he had seen at many fairgrounds and travelling circuses. She did not sit but instead stood facing the audience. Behind her was a table spread with an array of various objects; a jug of water and a glass, a comb and a brass-handled mirror among other things.

She proceeded to amaze the crowd with mind tricks, making one volunteer drink the water, convinced it was vinegar, causing him to retch and spew to a roaring applause. A woman was brought forth and made to believe that she was a barber and proceeded to comb and cut an imaginary person's hair whilst the audience howled with laughter. Another man was brought up to the stage and after a few suggestions in Miss Buki's hypnotic voice, became so terrified of his own reflection in the mirror that he cowered and cried for mercy.

At last Miss Buki bowed. The audience bellowed out their approval and the roof was almost lifted by their applause. The gypsy lady swept offstage and Mary turned to Lazarus, regarding him expectantly. "Not too shabby, eh?"

"Not at all," he agreed. "Very entertaining."

"Miss Buki is a good friend of mine. When I came to London she was my only friend, really. She took me under her wing and got me my first lodgings. Come on. I'll introduce you."

They got up and followed Mary through the crowd as the manager presented the following act; a pair of young women whose special ability involved the lifting of heavy weights by their teeth. They went back out into the lobby and through a side door that led backstage.

Miss Buki was to be found in a small dressing room barely large enough to contain the table and chair that occupied it, much less four visitors.

"Mary, is that you, *chavi*?" she said, rising.

"Hello, Miss Buki," Mary replied.

"Welcome, my dear, welcome! And your friends too!"

They squeezed into the little room and Mary and Miss Buki embraced. The room was stuffed full of various artifacts pertaining to its occupier's vocation. As well as the usual gypsy knick-knacks, there were a surprising number of books piled up on shelves, diverse in subjects from history to science. Rolls of paper sketched with spidery diagrams of the brain and the human anatomy were stacked up loosely, and an alarmingly real-looking skull peered down from a top shelf. All in all, the room gave the impression of belonging to a surgeon with a flair for colorful trinkets.

"Well, my dear," said Miss Buki, catching Lazarus surveying her quarters. "You look a little surprised."

"I must confess that I am, Miss Buki," he said. "I

had expected something a little... different. I see you have a keen interest in the scientific."

"The study of the mind is as fine a science as that of plants or animals," she replied. "Unfortunately, it's a study little recognized by institutions or the greater public, who show more care for witchcraft and crystal balls. Don't be fooled by my performance on stage for it is naught but science boiled off to simple tricks to amuse a crowd, akin to using a Brougham to pull firewood. It's a sad fact that I must keep up the pretence of mysticism and mummery to display a purer science that would be better suited to lecture halls and universities. But I have done my best to keep the charlatanism to a minimum. No bloody crystal balls I said to the manager when he hired me. I ain't no stick and rag show. But that's all people want though. Bloody crystal balls and tarot cards. And I don't do no dukkering neither, I said. If people want their palms read then they can bugger off to any old fairground come the summer months."

"Then you are not a real gypsy?" asked Mansfield.

The woman frowned at him, showing some offence. "I most certainly am, mister! I was born to the clans of Kent though my family has its roots in Hungary. I have roamed far a-field in my time, with the caravans of the eastern steppes where the black forests meet snow-capped mountains, and there is no river in England that I have not voyaged down. Gypsy I am, and proud of it too. But it is late and I am tired. You had better tell me what you are here for, so I can see if I may be of any service."

"Miss Buki," Lazarus said. "We have come to you on account of my friend Mansfield here. He is very troubled and we wish to call upon your skills as a mesmerist to ascertain the cause of his torment."

Miss Buki turned to Mansfield and fixed her beady eyes on him. "I'm not a doctor, lad."

Mansfield cleared his throat with discomfort. "I… uh… ahem, I have troubled sleep. Sometimes I wake up in places without knowing how I got there. I have done terrible things without any memory of doing them. It's like a part of my personality takes over involuntarily. I feel that there is an evil presence inside of me struggling to break through. I fear that I may not be able to contain it."

"Really?" said Miss Buki with raised eyebrows. "That is most interesting. I have heard of these so called double-personalities but have never met anybody with the condition."

"Then I am not alone?" Mansfield asked, his eyes glimmering with hope. "There are others? It is a condition then, and I am not merely a lunatic!"

"One man's lunatic is another man's prophet," said Miss Buki sagely. "It is often a matter of opinion. But yes, there have been documented cases of individuals displaying more than one personality, sometimes up to three or four, all fighting for control of their soul."

"Is it possible to communicate with any one of these personalities without the others interfering?" Lazarus asked her. "Like in a séance?"

"A séance?" Miss Buki remarked, the corners of her lips turning up in a smile. "This is a science, sir, not a parlor trick. But you are right in one thing; our understanding of the human mind is akin to our understanding of the cosmos in that we may only peek around the corner and make assumptions on what we may see. Hypnotism can be used to bring one personality to the fore but whether or not the others will stand idly by, I cannot say. Nor can I say with any certainty that hypnotism will work at all."

"But will you try on Mansfield?"

"Gladly, if only out of my own interest in this rare disease."

"Mary, would you leave us?" Lazarus asked.

She turned to him in surprise. "Leave? Why?"

"This is a very personal and private matter for Mansfield. He would be embarrassed to reveal so much of himself to you. Please allow Mr. Clumps to accompany you."

"I am to leave too?" the mechanical asked.

"I wouldn't want Miss Kelly to be left unattended in such surroundings," Lazarus told him.

Mary rolled her eyes. "A chaperone? Such a gent. But you do realize what I do for a living?"

Lazarus gave her a pleading look.

"Oh, all right. But I don't see what the bleedin' fuss is about. We'll be just outside waiting for you."

Once they had gone, Lazarus turned to the gypsy woman. "There is one other thing before we begin, Miss Buki. My friend often takes to raving and displaying violence when his darker nature consumes him. Is there somewhere we may go where he could be restrained?"

She eyed them both carefully. "Is he dangerous?"

"Possibly."

"Hmm. Come with me." She led them out of her dressing room and down a set of steps into a gloomy basement room filled with packing crates. "That's the thing we want in the corner there," she said, indicating a flat board stood upright between two cases. "You lads bring it out here where we have some space."

It was heavy, and after a bit of grunting and

dragging, they managed to heave the thing into the centre of the room. It had a hefty metal base from which protruded a lever that altered the angle of the board. Miss Buki instructed them to set it to forty-five degrees. Manacles dangled from its corners and a thick leather belt hung loose at the middle. For all the world it looked like a machine of terrifying torture, or perhaps a piece of medical equipment from Bedlam.

"This was used some time ago as part of a conjuror's act," explained Miss Buki. "He would ask a member of the audience to chain him up, and then he would wriggle free in under a minute. But don't worry. Unless your friend here is a master of escape, he shan't be getting free without our help."

Mansfield looked acutely uneasy as he stepped up onto the device and Miss Buki fixed the leather belt and manacles on him. Lazarus was far from comfortable himself and admired his friend's courage and trust in this woman.

Once her willing volunteer was fully secure, the hypnotist stepped back and began her slow, sleek talk, with suggestive references to calm beaches, trickling rivers and all the beautiful and peaceful things in life. Mansfield's eyelids began to droop as he fell deep into slumber, just as Lazarus had seen the three audience members do upstairs.

"Open your eyes, please," said Miss Buki, "and tell me whom I have the pleasure of addressing."

Mansfield slowly opened his eyes, saying nothing, and for an instant, Lazarus feared that the process had not worked. Then the man on the table tried to move and, finding himself restrained, unleashed a barrage of enraged jerks and heaves, yanking at the chains and writhing in the leather corset. The person called

Mansfield had totally vanished, leaving only the expression of a demon before them who fixed a terrible stare full of loathing upon Miss Buki.

"Is your name Mansfield" Miss Buki asked and Lazarus silently commended her for retaining her composure in the face of such a caged animal.

"Fuck off, witch!" said the creature in a voice as chilling as icy cold water running over sharp rocks.

"Are you Mansfield?" she repeated.

The man barked a cruel laugh. "I am not, but he is chained to me as I am to him and as both of us are to this infernal gurney! I am Mansfield's rage, his pain and his anger. I am his fear, his loathing and his hatred!"

"Why have you taken up residence in his body?"

"I have always been there, just as I am in every single person, since the human race crawled from apedom. I am their evil, their malice and their secret desire for all things unclean and degenerate. In a manner of speaking, I am Satan!"

Lazarus stepped forward, angry. "Do you make him kill, you bastard?" He felt Miss Buki turn her eyes upon him suddenly.

The creature looked at Lazarus with its black pupils. "A mere side effect. Unfortunate for them, but intensely gratifying for us. The whores were not part of the plan, but Mansfield so enjoys the exotic things in life. Now, with me by his side, he has been able to fulfill his desires to the maximum. He has such a hatred for those tarts that it almost rivals his love for them. Did you know that his father died of syphilis?"

"What side effect?" Lazarus asked. "What plan?"

With that, the creature began to giggle manically.

"Who are you?" Miss Buki demanded. "Do you have a name?"

The creature ceased its mirth and then spoke with deadly sincerity. "My name is Hyde!"

Try as they might, they could get no further sense out of him. Miss Buki used her calming technique to send the creature back into the darkest parts of Mansfield's mind and eventually Lazarus's friend returned to them, sobbing with exhaustion.

"What have you brought me here, mister?" Miss Buki asked Lazarus. She looked frightened. "What was all that about murder? In God's name sir, is this the Whitechapel killer?"

"Yes," Lazarus replied. "And no. As you can see, there is more than one person within the man before us. I must ask you to keep this to yourself, Miss Buki. I want to cure my friend, but if you breathe a word of this to anyone it will be the gallows for him or the rest of his life in Colney Hatch."

Miss Buki nodded slowly. "I also believe that there is more to this. His mind seems to have been… *tampered* with. Perhaps someone else with my skills has conditioned his mind in such a manner that murder flourishes from his fingertips."

"Is that possible?"

"Certainly. People can be set in motion much like machines, with the right knowhow. You have heard of those poor creatures in the Americas? They call them mechanicals but they were people once, just as you and I."

"Yes. Before their bodies were corrupted by machinery."

"Not just their bodies. Their minds, too. How else do you think they blindly follow the orders of the monsters who mutilated them? Their minds have been altered beyond repair so that they are no more than puppets dancing on invisible strings. Both the United and Confederate States employ scientists far more accomplished than I to corrupt the minds of their subjects and create an army of hollow slaves."

"Like the zombis of Africa," Lazarus said.

"Exactly."

"God, I wonder what was done to poor Mansfield, and by who?"

"And to what purpose?" added Miss Buki.

"Why would anyone condition a man to kill prostitutes? It doesn't make any sense."

"But he said that the killings were just a side effect and weren't part of the plan."

"Plan," Lazarus mused aloud. "What plan? Is there no way we can undo what was done to him?"

She shook her head. "He is not totally beyond salvage, for he is his own man most of the time with this Hyde character lurking just beneath the surface. But without knowing what signal sets him off, we have no way of stopping it taking control. I suggest that you remove him from his normal environment. That way you may be able to cut him off from the stimulus. You must promise me that you will do this, for the love of God! Don't let him kill again or I will be forced to tell what I know."

"I'll arrange something. What was that you said about a stimulus?"

"Whenever somebody is hypnotized there is always a stimulus keyed in to make them react. You saw me snapping my fingers on stage to bring those poor fools back to us. It works in reverse too; I can condition a man to act a certain way in response to a stimulus."

"What other kinds of stimuli are there other than snapping fingers in their faces?"

"Oh, anything really. Usually it is sounds, but it can be sights and smells too. Any sensory input."

Mansfield groaned.

"Let's get him loose from this thing," Lazarus said. Mrs. Buki seemed reluctant. "Come now, woman, Hyde has retreated for now. He's harmless, I promise you."

"You place a great deal of trust in your friend," she said as they loosened the manacles and the belt. "One can't help but wonder if you had not trusted him so in the first place, some of those poor girls might have been saved."

Chapter Eleven

In which an investigation begins

November 25th, 1863

After an unremarkable couple of days that tested my patience to the extreme, I am finally up and about. I have so much to report that I have neither pencil nor pages sufficient to write it all down, and so I must push ahead with a description of the place I find myself in.

It is a city in every sense of the word, clinging to the mountains like moss in the cracked face of a boulder. The majority of its houses are of simple bamboo construction much like elsewhere in Siam, but the heart of the city is a complex of stone buildings that comprise the royal palace and 'wat' or temple. It is a place the like of which I and, I may hazard a guess, even Henri Mouhot, would have doubted the existence of, for it hearkens back to a distant era in Siam's history.

The entrance faces east and is of huge wooden doors, brightly painted. In fact, the citadel is of exquisite artifice. White lime-coated walls ring it, with roofed galleries of terracotta tiles painted in blues and greens. The temple is of five towers in the shape of beehives that rise up higher than the whole city, plated in gold leaf so that they glitter like gilded honey drizzlers. I have been told by Kasemchai that these five towers represent the five peaks of Mount Meru in Hindoo mythology. But this is no relic of Siam's old religion, converted to the Buddhist faith like so many others in this land and in neighbouring Cambodia. The king and the people who dwell in this mountain stronghold are indeed Hindoos; remnants of the old religion who, due to their seclusion and cunning ways, have remained unchanged by the conversion of the whole of South East Asia to Buddhism.

As soon as it was known that I was well enough to be up and about, I was taken to the royal palace for an audience with the king. I was led to a carpeted audience chamber where a good number of officials crawled around on the floor in the manner of the Siamese in the presence of royalty. Kasemchai was by my side to act as translator, for nobody in this mountain city speaks English or French. We prostrated ourselves but as soon as my forehead touched the carpet the king bade me rise.

King Harshavarman is in his forties, strong-looking but he is at present struck by some malady which means he is unable to rise from his throne, or even his bed some days. His bald head is often beaded with sweat and he sometimes doubles over as if in great abdominal pain.

His condition did not prevent him from thanking me profusely for saving the life of his eldest son and heir, Prince Ksitindraditya, and presenting me with the skin of the beast I had slain with my improvised bamboo spear. It lies at the foot of my bed as I write this, and I look forward to bringing it back to Bangkok to see what Michael makes of it.

My audience with the king was short, as he is very ill indeed today and had to be taken back to his bedchamber while the palace physician was called for. The rest of the day was taken up by a tour of the citadel, including the great temple which really is a building of remarkable workmanship.

Every surface of its interior is covered with intricate carvings depicting scenes from the Ramayana, images of Shiva (the god to whom the temple is dedicated) astride his bull, Nandin, and episodes from the life of the earliest ruler of this city who built the temple and palace. He must have been a great visionary, or at least had some very cunning architects for the blocks of stone that comprise the temple are smooth as glass and are fitted together seamlessly so it appears as if the whole building is a single block of stone, hollowed out and carved with its decorations. Only the drilled holes found in some blocks indicate the method used in hauling them into place.

Kasemchai, translating the words of our guide, gave me a little lesson on the history of this fascinating city. Founded sometime (as close as I can guess) in the twelfth century by European reckoning, the 'Midnight City', as it translates to in our tongue, was one of the furthest and most remote temple cities of the Khmer Empire. Its secluded location retained its religion and independence during Siam's following centuries of upheaval. It survived the Lao kingdom of Lan Xang, the rise of the Sukhothai and Ayutthaya empires and the eventual domination of the current kingdom of Siam.

The kings of the Midnight City have long held the belief that their survival lies in independence and isolation through secrecy. I was alarmed to learn that I am the first white man ever to be admitted to the citadel, and it was only through my saving of Prince Ksitindraditya's life that I am allowed here at all. Kasemchai seems to be their only contact with the outside world.

A great trust has been bestowed upon me in letting me into their lost world. Our guide tells us that King Harshavarman fears that should his existence become known to King Mongkut, he would be forced to become a vassal and his daughters would end up in the latter king's harem. It is therefore a secret I will carry with me to my grave and pray that my private journal never falls into anybody else's hands. This is for my diversion only and when I am old and grey I will destroy these papers.

As soon as they got back to their lodgings in Limehouse, Lazarus sent Mr. Clumps to the nearest chandlers to purchase several lengths of chain.

"Is he dangerous, then?" Mary asked, eying the slumbering Mansfield on the bed, drowsy once again after his recent episode.

"You've been good to us, Mary," Lazarus said, "and you deserve an explanation. My friend is very ill. Miss Buki used her hypnotism on him and we discovered that he has another personality within him that occasionally fights its way to the fore."

"Another personality?" said Mary, struggling to understand. "Like a secret life?"

"More than that. He has no idea of what he says or does when his other personality takes over."

"How queer..."

"Sometimes he becomes... energetic and must be restrained."

"Are you sure he doesn't belong in Bedlam?"

"No, of that I am not sure. But he's my friend and I want to try and help him before I have to make that drastic decision. Bedlam and its ilk are terrible places. But I need your further help, if you're willing to give it."

"I dunno, it seems a bit dangerous..."

"I promise that he is no threat to you. Why, I cannot explain, but I am hoping that together we can find out."

"What do you need me for?"

"I need your knowledge of other ladies in your profession, specifically in Whitechapel. What they do, how they act, how they smell..."

"Smell?"

"I don't mean to be crude. You smell very lovely, I must say. But there is something that triggers Mansfield's episodes and it is something about the women in Whitechapel. Maybe something about the places in which they, um, conduct their business transactions. Maybe it is a personal possession they all hold in common. Maybe it is something they all say, a slang term perhaps, that sparks off his mania."

"Let me get this straight," said Mary very slowly. "Something we Whitechapel bag-tails do, or say, or own, makes your friend here go off on one? Why am I safe? How do you know that I won't 'spark off his mania' or whatever it is?"

"Because if you could then you would have done so already. No, there is something that only some working girls have in common, not all." He fumbled around in a drawer for a pencil and paper and a bundle of newspaper clippings. Mary watched him in silence as he began to write down some addresses, referring to the clippings frequently. "You understand that I only ask you to help me for time is so short. Ordinarily I would conduct my own investigations, but Mansfield's life hangs on our swift action."

"You talk an awful lot like a copper," she said, rising. She looked over his shoulder at the names and addresses he was scribbling down. "Polly Nichols - 56 Flower and Dean Street, Elizabeth Stride - 32 Flower and Dean Street, Catherine Eddowes - Casual Ward in Shoe Lane." She stopped and her eyes grew wide. "I knew it," she said, her voice a hoarse whisper. "He's the Ripper isn't he? My God, you've got me in a room with the bloody Ripper!"

"Mary, wait!" Lazarus cried as she bolted for the door, flung it open and rushed out into the street. He fumbled with his key to secure the door behind him, not for a second considering leaving Mansfield—*the Ripper*—alone and unsecured in a Limehouse bedsit.

Mary clattered down the street, her boots carrying her across the cobbles at a breakneck speed. Lazarus hurried after her. He couldn't let her go now, not with what she knew. She was probably on her way to the police station. Within an hour the news would be all over London that Mansfield was the killer. He *had* to stop her.

"Wait!" he cried again, seizing her by the elbow and spinning her around. She struggled to get free but he pinned her against a wall plastered with advertisements, aware of her similar manhandling at the hands of another man the day they had met. "Please hear me out!"

"You're as mad as he is!" she cried. "Sheltering that monster! And I helped you! Oh, Lord, you played me for a dolt, didn't you? Find a dim-witted bag-tail and trick her into helping the very man who all women despise, is that the game?"

"No! I wasn't sure Mansfield was the killer until the night of the double murder. There was no ulterior motive to my befriending you. Just two paths in this dreadful city crossing for a moment and in that moment two souls seeing a friend in the other, I swear! Now I beg you not to do anything rash. If you breathe a word of what you know it will mean the death of my friend. And I believe my friend to be innocent!"

"Innocent! Have you not read your little clippings? Have you not read of how he carved them up? Of how he ripped out their guts and scattered them about? And these were women like me! Women I have passed in the street, shared dosshouses with, shared punters with. How can you say with any certainty that I'll not be next?"

"Because he hasn't shown the slightest interest in you!"

"And that's supposed to make me feel safe, is it?"

"I told you that he requires some sort of stimulus—a sight or a smell or a sound—and that is a stimulus that you have not provided."

"Not yet. But we don't know what the bloody stimulus is! I might do something tomorrow or the day after that'll have him after me with his knife!"

"Then help me find out what that stimulus is. Help me to help him and we can bring his madness to an end as well as his reign of terror over the streets of Whitechapel."

"What would you have me do?"

He handed her the slip of paper. "Go to these addresses. Question the people the victims lodged with. Ask about their habits, of any odd traits; anything that might set them apart from you and the other women of Whitechapel. They'll trust you, you're not the police. And you'll be finding out things the police won't have thought of. That's what's most important; anything that the police might have dismissed as irrelevant."

"And what will you be doing?"

"I'll be visiting the crime scenes to see if I can dig anything up there that might be of use."

"Wrong. You'll be making bloody well sure that that friend of yours stays in his bed and doesn't get up to his old tricks again. Because if he kills again, Mr. Longman, I'll peach on both of you so that you'll both swing!"

Her temporary silence was good enough for

Lazarus. It bought him some time at least, and who knew what she might turn up? She'd have a damned better chance at getting answers from the women in those dosshouses than he or the police did.

When he returned to the bedsit, he found Mr. Clumps standing outside with the chain he had been sent to purchase.

"Has your friend gone home?" the mechanical asked.

"Yes," Lazarus replied. "Help me get Mansfield secured."

Mansfield was not happy about being chained up like a mad dog, but he begrudgingly accepted it as necessary. "How long am I to remain here in your lodgings?" he asked Lazarus. "I am due to perform again in two days."

"I'm afraid Mr. Hyde will have to be put on ice for a while," Lazarus told him. "In more ways than one. I'll get a message to Stoker."

"It'll ruin the company..."

"There are far greater things at stake here."

"Yes, you're quite right."

"I'll not rest until I find out the root of your madness, Richard," Lazarus told him. "We'll have you back on stage in no time."

True to his word, Lazarus wasted no time and was out that night, scouring the scenes of murder in Whitechapel. But he found that the only thing they had in common was their squalid and neglected appearances and the fact that all were dark, out of the way places where a woman would have to be mad or desperate to venture into with an unknown man.

Buck's Row was narrow and shaded by warehouses. The lettering on one wall read; 'Browne & Eagle'. The other side of the street was lined by a shabby two-storey terrace with dulled, curtained windows.

The back yard of 29 Hanbury Street where the body of Annie Chapman was discovered was filled with junk and broken furniture. The fence against which her body had been dumped was ramshackle and crooked. Lazarus could detect the yeasty smell of the Black Eagle Brewery over on Brick Lane.

Mitre Square was reached by a gloomy, narrow entrance called Church Passage. Warehouses of three or four stories faced it on all sides. 'Kearly & Tonge' was spelled out in large letters on the side of one of them.

Lazarus noted all of this down. It was late. Prostitutes were propositioning him and men were eying him suspiciously, as well they might eye anybody walking around Whitechapel with a pencil and notepad in the middle of the night. He decided to leave Dutfield's Yard until tomorrow. He could have a snoop around there when he went over to the club in the morning.

When he got back, he decided to try out a few things on Mansfield. His friend was awake and, still chained to the bed, was accepting a cup of tea courtesy of Mr. Clumps who was holding it up to Mansfield's lips in one massive paw.

"He doesn't make a bad cuppa," Lazarus said, taking over from the mechanical who shambled over to the fire and poked at the glowing coals.

"Not too bad, although you boys could do with owning a strainer," said Mansfield, spitting out a tealeaf onto the blanket.

"Richard, I'd like to try a few experiments on you."

Mansfield sighed. "I don't think I'm up to it, old

boy. I can't cope with another episode, not two in one day."

"I know it's hard on you but we must try to isolate the cause of your episodes. I've been out collecting potential stimuli. Now, let's see..." he held up his pad with the words 'Browne & Eagle' and 'Kearly & Tonge' written in block capitals. Mansfield stared at them with a blank expression.

"Nothing? Hmm." The yeasty smell from the Black Eagle brewery was something else he'd like to try and would see about getting hold of some fermenting beer later in the day. But for now, it was best that they all got a little rest. As the cot was occupied, he bedded down on the floor with his blanket around him.

Chapter Twelve

In which an ointment of foreign origin is purchased

November 26th, 1863

I spent the early part of the day sketching the carvings and bas reliefs of the citadel. This is a little out of my area of expertise and it feels strange to be sketching manmade images instead of the works of nature. I can only imagine what a fine study Henri Mouhot would make of all of this. But as he is dead and there is likely to be no other white man admitted to this mountain stronghold, I must do my best to record all as best I can. But good God, there is not enough lead in my pencil nor strength in my arm to record all this wonderful city has to offer!

Kasemchai came to me a little after lunch. "King very sick," he said.

I replied that I had been made aware of the fact during our audience with his majesty yesterday.

"Worse today," Kasemchai said. "If he die then we must leave very quickly."

"Why?" I asked.

"Many here do not like white man in Midnight City. If king die then we may die with him."

"But surely Prince Ksitindraditya will ensure that we come to no harm. He will be king if Harshavarman dies, yes?"

"Maybe. Maybe not. Noblemen do not like king or his son. Maybe mutiny if he die."

I began to understand the gravity of the situation. Any kind of coup in the wake of the king's death could prove very problematic for us. I decided to find out more about the king's health. I am no doctor, but perhaps it was some mild malady easily remedied? I told Kasemchai to take me to the palace, where we interviewed several of the king's court as to the nature of his majesty's illness.

I was told that the king's illness was not a contagious one and was suffered by him alone. No wound caused it and it had only troubled him for a month or so. It was (the attendants believed) a punishment from the gods.

I demanded to be taken to the royal kitchens to examine his majesty's food preparations. I was not sure that he was being poisoned, but the symptoms suggested some dietary cause. I cannot for the life of me understand why they do not employ a food taster.

His majesty's diet is a fairly plain one considering his station in life. Pork, poultry, mountain river fish and rice seem to be the bulk of it with little flavourings but for lemongrass, Lao Coriander and several native flowers. I examined these and recognised Bombax ceiba and Sesbania grandiflora, but there was also a white blossom which I did not recognize as a flower often used for culinary purposes. I asked one of the cooks what it was and he told me it was pear blossom.

"No," I said. "Not pear blossom. These are too tubular." I had an uncomfortable feeling as I examined them. They had been chopped up, but by looking at some of the larger pieces I could imagine how they looked on the branch and I gradually came to the conclusion that they were from the Strychnos nux-vomica tree; the source of the deadly poison called strychnine.

"Very poisonous!" I warned them all. "These are making the king sick!"

The blossoms do not contain as much poison as the seeds of the tree which are known as 'Quaker Buttons' but whoever is poisoning the king obviously wants his death to appear as the result of a long sickness rather than murder.

The palace guard—who are female, I must add—were promptly called for and they were all for dragging the cooks to a court of execution until I intervened. "Very easy to mistake for pear blossoms," I instructed Kasemchai to translate. My guide was showing signs of reluctance to get involved, but I would not let three innocent men be executed for something that, in all probability, was not their fault. "Whoever wants the king dead probably slipped these into the kitchens in place of pear blossoms."

This seemed to pacify the guard and had the three cooks wailing their thanks for my intervention on their behalf. The episode brought me to the attention of the city's prime minister and I have just come back from another audience with the king and his most trusted circle of advisors.

The king thanked me once again for my services to him and I was permitted to remain and sit in on the council with Kasemchai translating. They were discussing how best to root out the traitor now that his plot to poison the king had been foiled and his majesty's health would soon be on the mend.

"Perhaps I may be permitted to make a suggestion," I told Kasemchai.

He looked at me askance. "Be careful," he said. "You are popular now but king is still king and you are a foreigner."

"But if his majesty would just hear me out..." I said, but our discussion had already caught the king's attention and he demanded to know what we were talking about.

"Your majesty," I said through Kasemchai. "One way to draw out the traitor is to make him think that his plan has succeeded." I was met with blank faces and so continued. "Make him think that your majesty has died and he will surely make his move with all haste. Then, like a Venus flytrap, you may close your jaws on him."

"A ruse?" the king replied, and he discussed this with his

councilors and prime minister. After a while he turned to me. "An excellent idea. We shall let this traitor think he has won and then, strike when he is overconfident."

There was much to prepare in the execution of the plan and so we left his majesty and his council to it. But even as I write this I can hear that the first part of the plan has been put into motion. The wails of the harem for their lost king echo through the palace. Tomorrow will be an interesting and possibly dangerous day.

Mary's eagerness to see an end to the Whitechapel murders did not disappoint Lazarus, for she knocked on their door early the next morning. While Lazarus had been playing detective at the various murder sites, she had spent the night visiting the dosshouses on Flower and Dean Street and the one in Shoe Lane. She hovered on the threshold, looking at Mansfield who sat propped up in bed, his arms bound with chains.

"You can come in," Lazarus said. "Mansfield is quite harmless."

She came in but sat on the chair near the door. "I'll just perch here if it's all the same to you."

"I don't blame you for mistrusting me, miss," said Mansfield.

"If I had my way you'd be locked up at Commercial Street Station right now," Mary replied. "Got any gin? I'm dead beat and my feet are killing me. I haven't a penny to my name neither with all the tramping about I've been doing instead of earning."

Lazarus fetched the bottle from the chest of drawers and poured her a glass. It was too early for him to join her but she didn't mind drinking alone, knocking it back and holding her glass out for another. "I got no money for rent, that's what really worries me. I'll be out on the street if I don't get back to work and put in some overtime."

Lazarus reached into his pockets and counted out some shillings for her. She looked at him without taking the coin. "It's not charity," he promised her. "I just don't want you getting into bother on my account."

"Well, all right. Let's call it my pay for doing your job for you."

"Did you find anything out?"

"Maybe. There was nothing at Flower and Dean Street, but there was a woman in the casual on Shoe Lane who knew Catherine Eddowes. I asked her all the stuff you told me; what was she like, how she dressed, and all. I also asked her if she had any personal belongings left over. The woman seemed a bit tight-lipped about it, but I pressed her and she told me that as the woman was dead now it didn't do no harm for her to have taken a few bits and pieces for herself."

"What sort of bits and pieces? Anything she didn't have with her when she was murdered won't be our stimulus."

"No, and for the most part it was just a comb, a bit of broken mirror and some undergarments. But I got to thinking what you said about smell. Well, we bag-tails have to be careful to avoid getting with child. Some syringe themselves out with a solution of zinc, alum, pearl ash and other nasty stuff after a man does his business. Some just use vinegar. Mesself, I just make a punter pull out before he reaches his jolly heights. Saves mess. Anyway, there's this new potion on the street what's become quite popular. I don't know what's in it. Probably just some jollop that does no good but it don't half pong. It's got some perfumed scent to it probably to cover up the smell of all the horrible stuff that's in it."

"And Catherine Eddowes used this stuff?"

"Must of done 'cos this woman I spoke to pinched a bottle of it from her after she died. What do you reckon? Is this what we're after?"

"It could be. But there's only one way to be sure. Mary, I want you to go and procure me a bottle of this stuff."

"All right, but if I bring it to you, you just let me get a good distance from here before you start waving it under his nose. I don't want to be anywhere near him when he turns."

"Absolutely."

As she opened the door to leave, she nearly bumped into a figure on the doorstep. It was Levitski. "Friend of yours?" Mary asked Lazarus as the Russian stood back to let her pass.

"An associate, yes," Lazarus replied.

Mary gave the Russian Jew a queer look before she headed off on her errand.

"Levitski," said Lazarus. "Good morning."

"Good morning, comrade," the Russian replied. "Had company last night?"

"No, she just stopped by for some breakfast. Her brother was a friend of mine before he got the cholera. I look after her from time to time."

"Very charitable of you. If only more Londoners were as selfless as you are, we wouldn't have need of bloody revolution."

"I'm surprised to see you so early, Levitski. I take it

you wish to go to the club?"

"I thought we might take a wander over to Victoria Park to hear Yoshka's new speech."

"Damn! I forgot! Apologies, comrade, I've had a busy time. I'll just get my coat."

"And comrade Clumps too?" Levitski tried to peer in and Lazarus quickly blocked his view. It would not do at all to let Levitski see Mansfield chained to his bed. That would take some explaining.

"Actually, he's feeling a bit under the weather. Had a little too much to drink last night. He won't be joining us."

"I see. Thought he had the constitution of an ox, that one. Very well, shall we be off?"

Lazarus left Mr. Clumps to care for Mansfield. He had to admit, the mechanical was turning out to be a perfect nurse.

They cut through Mile End and passed a tailor's that had recently seen some violence. The pavement glistened with broken glass and a woman sat cradling a man's bloodied head. She was weeping. The name above the broken window was a Jewish one.

"What the devil happened here?" said Lazarus.

"There's been attacks all over the East End," said Levitski. "Against Jewish businesses. People beaten up. It started in Whitechapel early this morning but has spilled over into other districts."

"Why?"

"The Ripper. The prejudiced press have everybody convinced it's a Jew that's the killer. Most people can't bring themselves to believe that an Englishman could be capable of committing such atrocities and that it has to be a foreigner. And the police are looking for a suspect nicknamed 'Leather Apron'. Well, everybody knows that most of the Jews in London wear leather aprons according to their trades as tanners and bootmakers."

"But that's madness!"

"Believe me, my friend, it takes but the tiniest of sparks to blow a powder keg. I have seen it in my homeland; prejudice and hatred will mount and mount until the barest whisper of suggestion breaks the dam."

As they headed further north, they appeared to be approaching the heart of the tension. Two more shops had been vandalized and an old Jew lay beaten and groaning in the street. Fortunately, his life had been saved by a quick rallying of his neighbors some of whom, Lazarus was relieved to see, were Englishmen who had chased the mob away.

"They're heading across Hamlet's Way," said one of them. "Watch yourselves."

"There'll be a bloody pogrom in East London at this rate," said Lazarus. "Where are the police?"

"Far from wherever they can be of any use, as usual," said Levitski.

They cut across Hamlet's Way and saw the wake of destruction left by the mob. There did seem to be a police presence after all, as a group of uniformed coppers came jogging around the corner and headed east.

"Come on," said Lazarus. "We don't want to go where they're headed, assuming they're even on the right track."

They nipped up a side street and noted how deathly quiet it was. Jewish businesses were boarded up with their owners barricaded inside. Other shops and homes had their curtains drawn, their inhabitants pretending that violence was not stomping up and down their streets.

They ducked into an archway and just before they reached the sunlight on the other side, the mob shambled into view. 'Mob' was a generous word for this group of ruffians. There were five or six of them, armed with bits of chain, lengths of wood and pipes. They appeared to have broken off from the main body of troublemakers to scour the side streets and alleys for easy pickings. In seeing Lazarus and Levitski, they clearly felt that they had found some.

"There's a pork-dodger!" cried one of them and they advanced with the slow pace of those who had the luxury of taking their time with their prey.

"Come on," said Levitski in a panicked voice, "back the way we came."

But the other end of the archway was blocked by two more ruffians who had snuck around from a side street. They grinned at their trapped prey.

"Just let us pass and there'll be no trouble," Lazarus told them.

"Oh, we *wants* trouble," said one of the men, testing the strength in the thick piece of wood he held in his hands. "*Race traitor*," he added, looking Lazarus up and down with distaste. "Don't you know it's bad for your health to be seen on these streets in the company of a Yid?"

Lazarus drew his Bulldog revolver and aimed it at the man who had spoken. It seemed to have a brief effect on the group, but their confidence in numbers quickly overcame their hesitation. The man with the club advanced. Lazarus squeezed the trigger and felled him with one shot. The thugs fell back, shocked by their prey's willingness to take a life.

"Back off," Lazarus warned them, chambering

another round and holding the gun on them.

The group reluctantly let them pass and soon Lazarus and Levitski were pounding down the street and around the corner, continuing northwards. They swung into a shop doorway and caught their breaths.

"Shit, comrade!" panted Levitski. "Do you always carry a cannon?"

"I'm a military man," Lazarus replied. "I've never felt safe without one. Whether it's mad Mahdists or East End villains, I'm always prepared."

"Do you see how the failure of the state and its corrupt police has left us with no option but to use violence to protect ourselves?" Levitski said.

"I'm surprised you don't carry a weapon."

"A Jewish anarchist with a concealed weapon quickly finds himself at the end of a rope," the Russian replied. "Our time for violence will come but for the meantime we must choose our battles and marshal our forces in secret."

"Is that how you see the club? The marshalling of forces? To me there is far too much talk going on in Berner Street and not enough action."

"Not enough people like you or I, you mean," said Levitski with a smile. "Too many philosophers and poets. Propaganda and speeches will only get us so far, we both know this. I have had my eye on you for some time now, comrade, and now I am convinced that you are of a caliber far greater than the rest of those soft heads at the club. I would like to introduce you to a select group of friends whose anarchist designs run much further than meeting *Arbeter Fraynd*'s next deadline."

"Are you a member of another club?"

"You might say that. But it is not the sort of club

where fellows sit around drinking tea and debating Babeuf and Fourier. We keep ourselves very low key. That is why I have not mentioned it to you before. I had to be sure your philosophies were sincere and that you were not a police plant or a government spy."

"You intrigue me, comrade."

"Then I shall take you to meet my friends."

"When?"

"I will call on you at an unspecified time, but you must be ready to leave and be gone for some days."

"Well, I have already lost my job at the docks so nobody will really miss me. But days? What could be so involving?"

"Merely one of our security measures. But there will be plenty to keep you occupied."

They continued to Victoria Park and heard out Yoshka's speech. It felt like their way of saying farewell to the Berner Street club and all its useless philosophers and poets.

When Lazarus got back to Limehouse he found Mr. Clumps entertaining Mary. She still preferred to sit by the door, as far away from the bed and its occupant as possible.

"Any luck?" he asked her.

"It's mayhem out there!" she said. "Gangs are tearing apart Whitechapel looking for your friend. They reckon it's a Jew."

"I know," Lazarus replied. "But you were not harmed?"

She snorted and tossed him a brown paper bag. "Here you are!"

It in was a little bottle of green glass with a typically vague label that read;

Dr. Schäfer's Female Remedy

A Preventative Wash for Married Women

New Recipe - Pleasing Aroma

Beware of Counterfeits

"Dr. Schäfer," murmured Lazarus. "Sounds German. I'm going to take this to a chemist and see if they can't find out what's in it. But first we need to test it on Mansfield."

"You remember what I said?" Mary said in a warning tone as she rose from the chair.

"Of course. You'd better be off then. Just be careful. You don't look Jewish but these mobs will take advantage of any distraction."

"Don't you worry. I've survived worse trouble than this."

"Will I see you again?"

"Depends if you need me for any more errands."

"Perhaps I will. Or perhaps I'll just drop by the *Ten Bells* for a drink with you sometime."

"I can't promise you I'll be there," she said. "But if I am, then yes, maybe we'll have a drink."

He watched her leave and then closed the door and turned to Mansfield. "Right, then, old friend. I know this is a rough business but we have to try."

"She's a lovely girl," said Mansfield. "You do what you have to to keep her and her kind safe from me."

"Right you are," said Lazarus. He uncorked the little bottle and took a whiff. It certainly was aromatic but he couldn't place it. It was a blend of many different scents that masked something acrid and chemical beneath. "Prepare yourselves," he said to his friends. And he held the bottle under Mansfield's nose.

Chapter Thirteen

In which a new society is joined

November 27th, 1863

I was not wrong about the perils my suggested plan to the king might entail. I barely slept a wink for the clamour of mourning sweeping the palace and descending into the city below. The lights of torches flickered in the night like fireflies as the city remained awake with me.

Before dawn somebody hammered on my door. I thought it would be Kasemchai but I opened it to find two of the king's bodyguards. They spoke to me in their own tongue with much gesticulating and, in frustration at my blank expression, hauled me from my chamber in a state of undress.

Alarmed to say the least at being dragged through the palace by a pair of ferocious Amazons, I realised that I was under some sort of arrest and thought it best to hold my tongue for the time being. We found the throne room in a state of great excitement. A man I did not recognise sat on the throne with the air of a cat that had devoured both the cream and the canary.

Noblemen summoned from their homes (with perhaps more dignity that I had been) prostrated themselves at his feet. There were many attendants at the arms of the usurper, many more than the true king usually had about him. They wore cloaks of maroon, covering their bodies so that they resembled monks of an exotic sort.

I was held in a vice-like grip by my two escorts like some sort of political prisoner about to be beheaded. My eyes darted around for any sign of Kasemchai but I could see none. Neither was there any sign of the true king or Prince Ksitindraditya. The current occupant of the throne was speaking in a loud voice that demanded the attention and respect of all in the room. He began pointing a thin finger at me and jabbing it to punctuate his increasingly angry monologue.

I found myself being dragged forward and forced to kneel at the feet of this usurper. I heard the sound of a blade being unsheathed behind me and I began to panic. Iron-hard arms held my own outwards in the eagle position and stifled my struggling. I felt certain that I was about to die and began to recite the Lord's Prayer under my breath.

The doors to the throne room swung open and several men swept into the room, causing a great stir of confusion among the assembled court. The arms of my startled Amazons relaxed slightly at this intrusion, and I was able to turn a little to get a better look.

My heart filled with relief. Striding through the doors like a lion returning to his den was King Harshavarman himself, with Prince Ksitindraditya by his side and a score of attendants behind him.

The alarmed nobles did not know what to do. Should they flee in terror at the sight of this ghost? Or accept him as flesh and blood? But which king should they bow to now?

All eyes were on the usurper, but he smiled as if he had expected the sudden resurrection of his enemy. At his command the robed attendants behind him threw aside their maroon garbs and brandished blades and short throwing spears. The scene had the feel of a trap that had just been sprung.

The true king's bodyguard, spurred into action by this threat to their leader whom they had thought dead until now, drew their own weapons and rallied to Harshavarman and the prince. Finding myself suddenly released from bondage, I scurried to the nearest wall and remained on my haunches while the war for the throne broke out all around me.

I need not go into detail of the blood spilled in that room today, for I have not the stomach for it. I need only say that the battle went poorly for King Harshavarman and his followers, much to my distress. The usurper (whom I have since learned is a discontented nobleman by the name of Jayavarthon) had a remote claim to the throne and wished to accelerate the natural course of succession. Upon the reports of the king's death, he had entered the palace and taken the throne without anybody to stop him. He somehow predicted the king's ruse and so had his armed troops disguised as attendants accompany him into the palace. His intention was to kill both the king and his son within the palace walls, along with anybody who might bring word of this treachery to the city beyond.

As I write this the battle still rages on through the corridors of the palace. Every single one of the king's Amazons have been called to the fight and to do their lord proud but Jayavarthon has called on his own allies from the city, no doubt claiming that some usurper is trying to block his path to the throne.

Currently the king has set up his base in a series of supply rooms that run off from the kitchens, which we have barricaded with everything we can find. We are outnumbered and I do not know how long we can survive before they break in and are upon us. Perhaps this will be my last entry. If I am to be knifed in my sleep then there are only a few words left to say; I love you, Sarah, and I love you Michael. I can only pray that I will see you both again.

"Well, now we know that this foreign ointment is the stimuli," said Mr. Clumps, placing a damp towel over

Mansfield's slumbering face.

"And we can both be thankful for the chains you procured," Lazarus replied, loosening his collar. The room was not hot but sweat ran down his neck, cold sweat, borne out of fear. The words spoken from the mouth of his friend had chilled him, as had the rage and the hatred he had seen in those eyes as he had thrashed and strained against his chains.

That afternoon he took the vial of liquid to a chemist on Pennyfields, whom he had learned occasionally ran toxicological analyses for the police. The chemist looked at the label with distaste. "There's a lot of this muck about," he said, turning the bottle over in his hands to see if there was a reverse label. "Typical. No mention of the ingredients. Do a woman more harm than good, most likely."

"I was hoping you could tell me what was in it," Lazarus said.

"We ordinary chemists don't sell this sort of thing. It's the type of jollop people flog in the market or the Chinese in their shops round here. Probably mixed up in somebody's cellar with whatever came to hand thrown in. I'll take a look at it. What's your interest?"

"I'm a private detective pursuing a case for a client. Their daughter used some of this and my client believes it may have harmed her."

"Sounds like a case for the police," said the chemist with a frown.

"It's just a theory for the moment, but if there's anything dangerous in it than I shall notify the police, have no worries as to that."

The chemist told him to come back the next day and so Lazarus returned home. Mansfield was awake and looking sicker than ever.

"I think it would be best if we removed you back to your hotel room," Lazarus told him.

"Chains and all?" the actor asked.

"That might raise a few suspicions. No, I think that we need to get you out of the East End and reduce the likelihood of you coming into contact with any woman who may be using this ointment. I can't imagine the ladies at the Langham are the types to resort to such precautions. At least we'll have to hope they aren't. It's a bit of a gamble but I think it's far safer than keeping you in Limehouse. God knows how many women are walking around whiffing of this stuff. Or their customers for that matter. Sex spreads scents just as it does disease."

Mansfield breathed deeply. "So I can return to normal life then. As normal as it can be after all of this."

"I would stay in your rooms as much as possible for the sake of caution," Lazarus told him. "I still have work to do. I shall be calling on you."

That evening Lazarus and Mr. Clumps unlocked Mansfield's chains and escorted him to Commercial Road, where they took a cab to the Langham Hotel. There they enjoyed a meal together and saw him safely to his room. He seemed to be in better spirits than he had been in days, possibly at the prospect of sleeping in a fine bed without the need for chains, or perhaps he was feeling confident that Lazarus was getting closer to rooting out the cause of his problem. Lazarus only hoped that he would not let his friend down.

"Isn't it a bit dangerous letting him go free?" Mr. Clumps asked Lazarus on their way back to Limehouse.

"Perhaps. But we can't keep him in Limehouse. For

a start the whole of the East End with its working girls must remain a no-go area to him now. And secondly, his presence would be a hindrance in the pursuit of our mission for the government. I must say that you've been awfully good about this whole business, Clumps. Playing nurse for my friend is hardly in your job description. And I thank you for your trust and silence."

"Don't mention it," the mechanical replied. "My job description is to do whatever you tell me."

"Right, well I'm sorry to have spent so much time on what is essentially a personal matter. But now we can get back to pursuing our real business in the East End."

"Do you have a new lead?"

"I hope so. Levitski has promised to introduce us to a few friends of his. Friends made of sterner stuff than our comrades at the Berner Street club."

The next day Lazarus dropped in on the chemist in Pennyfields.

"A solution of Zinc and alum mixed with a watered down cologne to mask the smell," the chemist told him. "Unfortunately I could not ascertain the type but I detected bergamot and patchouli oils as well as sandalwood."

"Thank you," said Lazarus. "This is a big help."

"I don't see how," the chemist replied. "Nothing dangerous in it at all. If your client's daughter was somehow injured, then it was not because of the contents of this bottle. Although that's to say nothing of its ineffectiveness. It's a scam, really, but not a dangerous one."

"But at least I can rule it out as the cause of my client's complaints," said Lazarus.

In fact he intended to track down pure forms of every ingredient the chemist had given him and test each and every one of them on Mansfield in the safety of his hotel room. By hook or by crook he would isolate the stimulus that drove him to murder.

The following day Levitski came for them.

"I have spoken of you to my comrades," he said. "And they think you would both make valuable additions to our army."

"Army?" Lazarus enquired.

"Just a term we like to use. For are we not truly at war? Has not the class battle been going on since the dawn of time?"

It was a misty morning that saw them leave Limehouse and head westwards towards Whitechapel. It was a walk Lazarus and Mr. Clumps had taken many a cold morning, when the warm and friendly interior of the Berner Street club with its hot tea and good company was a welcome beacon to the hard up, unemployed workers of East London. But this time they veered north, crossing first Commercial Street, then Whitechapel Road. They were near Buck's Row, and it was on the street that lay between the site of Polly Nichol's murder and the Whitechapel and Mile End Station that their destination lay.

Several small dwellings were squashed close together, as if the hulking brickwork of the nearby Harrison, Barber & Co. Horse Slaughterers was forcing its weight against them. Levitski led them to the front door of a tenement with boarded up windows and peeling green paint. He rapped three times and a woman opened it.

She had dark hair and drawn, pinched features that made her seem older than her slender, shapely figure suggested. She said something to Levitski in Russian.

"My companions here do not speak our tongue, Anna, so we must be polite," he replied.

"Of course," said the woman, donning a smile. "My name is Anna Winberg and you are most welcome."

They were admitted to a rundown dwelling that had unfurling carpets and the barest essentials in the way of amenities. The smell of boiling cabbage and some sort of meat came from a small kitchen that led off from the living room. A coal fire burned in the grate, and above the chipped and cracked mantle was a portrait of Karl Marx. On the opposite wall was a cheap painting of some landscape in Eastern Europe.

Several men and women were seated around the fire on mismatched furniture. They wore greasy caps and coarse clothes, and had the red-rimmed eyes and calloused looks Lazarus knew from factory and sweatshop workers.

"Comrades," said Anna Winberg, addressing the assembled group, "meet our new friends from the Berner Street club."

"How do you do?" Lazarus said.

There were nods of acknowledgement all round.

"What's with the mask?" one of them said to Mr. Clumps. "None of us are wearing masks."

"Phossy jaw," Clumps said automatically.

"We're not vain types here," said another of the men. "We accept each other as comrades, warts and all."

"Some have more than a few warts," said Lazarus. "And some are even more unfortunate than you." He was annoyed by the rude treatment of his friend.

"Now then, comrades," said Levitski. "I know these two. They've got hearts true to the cause. There's no need for distrust if I vouch for them, no?"

"There'll be ample time to get to know one another over the next few days," said Anna. "Let's eat and then we'll head off."

"Head off where?" Lazarus asked.

"To our headquarters," Anna replied.

"But I thought..."

"This is just a way station," said Levitski. "A sort of ferrying point for new recruits into our world."

Over the course of the overcooked meal, Lazarus discovered that they were not the only 'new recruits' that morning. A metal worker called Ivan looked as bewildered by the whole arrangement as Lazarus felt, although his youth let it show more. There was also a seamstress called Ivy, no doubt culled from one of the sweatshops with promises of fierce reprisal against the system that imprisoned her. She was as mousy as her companion, and Lazarus had to wonder what use the revolution had for such meek individuals.

As promised, as soon as they had mopped up their plates with their crusts of dry bread, they were led through a locked door into a back room that was filled with rubble. This detritus had come from a gaping aperture that had been chiseled out of the brick wall at the rear of the house. Where this led, Lazarus hadn't the faintest idea. He had seen similar tricks used in America by robbers who let a property neighboring a bank, and then bore through the wall to pilfer at will after closing hours.

One by one, without explanation, they ducked into the dark aperture. The passage was not a long one, and after a bit of shuffling and feeling their way along, they emerged in a large room that had once been some sort of ticket office. Booths with dusty and cracked glass loomed in the shadows. Levitski lit a lamp and the light fell on walls plastered with advertisements several years out of date. A large railway clock lay in the centre of the room where it had fallen some years ago, its sad face thick with dust. The corner of a sign that had been removed and shoved behind some upturned benches read; 'Whitechapel'.

"This is the old station!" Lazarus exclaimed. "From before they merged Whitechapel with Mile End."

"Yes," Levitski replied. "This place has been abandoned since 1884."

"I had no idea it was still here."

"Funny," said Ivy the seamstress. "Fancy all this stuff just lying around in here all these years."

"You'd be amazed at how much stuff is forgotten beneath the city," said Anna.

"The way down is a long one," said Levitski, leading the group towards the stairwell above which the sign for 'To the Platform' still hung. "The old East London Railway line was one of the deeper ones."

With his lamp dancing off the green tiles, they descended the stairs that vanished ahead into blackness. The way was occasionally obscured by refuse tossed down there by the workers who had closed the place up four years ago. Rats scurried out of their way.

"So how did you end up with this lot then?" Lazarus asked the seamstress.

"Miss Winberg helps run a home for girls with no homes or families," Ivy replied. "Most of us are seamstresses who got ill or injured in the sweatshops.

They're a Godsend at that place. Hot meals, clean beds and friendly company. I'd be on the street if it weren't for Miss Winberg and her friends. Or worse."

"Don't you have any family?"

"Not since I was a little girl. Luckily my mum taught me how to sew so I escaped the workhouse and got a job as a seamstress on Goulston Street. Though I dunno which is worse. We were worked nearly to death at that place. Miss Winberg and her friends are my family now."

Lazarus was silent. Anna Winberg was clearly a procuress for London's destitute females, as Levitski was for its males. The question was, why? Why lure homeless, jobless folk down underground to join this elusive 'revolution'? He could understand Levitski bringing fellow socialists, disillusioned with the plodding pace of the Berner Street club, into his odd underground sect but why poor creatures like Ivy who likely as not couldn't read, let alone spout socialist rhetoric?

"What about you?" he asked Ivan the metalworker. "Do you have family?"

"No," the Russian replied. "I came here two years ago on my own. I was robbed on the docks by a gang of Englishmen who claimed to help newcomers to these shores. They took me to a house in Shadwell and said I could use my coat and clothes as a guarantee against a loan to pay for my bed. This was just until I found a job and could afford the three shillings a week. One of the gang promised to take me around the East End to get me work. He charged five shillings a day for this service, which was added to my tab. Soon enough I was out on the street without even the luggage I brought with me. I lived off handouts from Jewish charities until I eventually found work in one of the factories. I was paid in lodgings and tea to begin with, until I learnt how to operate the machines. Then I got four shillings a week for working from six in the morning to eleven at night. I couldn't cope and that's when Levitski found me."

Lazarus was no longer under any illusions as to Levitski's purpose at Berner Street. He had to wonder how many other workers and socialist clubs the Russian was a member of, or charities for that matter. He and Anna were like wolves, prowling the city's underbelly for new recruits for whatever it was that was going on down beneath the streets. Both Ivy and Ivan had no families. That probably explained why they had been chosen. *Nobody to miss them.*

They were down to the platform now, Levitski's lamp shooting their shadows across the curved walls of the tunnel. They hopped down onto the rails and headed into the blackness. On and on they journeyed, plunging deeper and deeper into the disused portions of the London Underground. Another tunnel joined theirs, and down its length they could see another lantern swinging as it approached. Levitski called out and was dually answered.

The strangers were dressed in similar working clothes and, much to Lazarus's alarm, they appeared to be armed. Two carried Berdan II single shot bolt-action rifles (favored by the Russian army) fitted with bayonets. Another carried a Martini-Henry and others were armed with pistols. For all the world they looked like guerrilla partisans here in the very heart of the British capital.

"Back from patrol?" Levitski asked them.

"The Doc has us scouring the exits at Greenwich

and the Docklands," replied one. "All shipshape. We're heading back now."

"You can check in with us then."

They walked along in silence. Lazarus knew he was not the only one who felt a little like they were now being escorted by an armed guard further into unknown territory. He also wondered who this 'Doc' was. *Their leader?* There came a gentle gust down the tunnel that ruffled their hair. Lights behind them, dim to begin with, rapidly grew in intensity, bathing them in light.

"Up against the wall, lads!" cried one of the armed men. "Hop to it!"

"By God!" Lazarus cried as the locomotive thundered towards them. He hurled himself against the curve of the wall and turned his face as it rushed past them, clattering and swaying. The armed men let out whoops of exhilaration in the thrill of danger. But for Lazarus, the terror of not knowing how close the sides of the carriages were from his face but feeling the air whooshing past in the blackness was like nothing he had ever felt before. Then, in an instant, it was gone; vanished into the gloom ahead.

"Everyone still with us?" Levitski asked, shining his lamp into their faces.

"What the bloody hell's the game here, Levitski?" Lazarus demanded, unable to contain his anger. "I thought this stretch of track was out of use."

"Goods trains still use it to get to Millwall Docks and Blackwall," Levitski replied. "But don't worry, we're nearly there."

They headed down a tunnel that branched off from the one the train had just passed through, and after a bit more walking they emerged into a wide cavern.

Lazarus was immediately put in mind of the underground base of Captain Townsend's Unionist Partisan Rebels deep beneath the Arizona Mountains.

It was made up of various sidings no longer in use. Brick pillars and arches gave the place a sepulchral feel, heightened by the regular gas lamps that cut everything up into angular patches of light and shade. People were everywhere, carrying supplies from horse drawn railway carts into rooms and chambers that led off from the platforms. Some lounged around cooking fires that glowed in little niches, boiling tea and soup and reading newspapers by the flickering orange light. They appeared to be soldiers, for they wore uniforms of grey and their weapons—rifles and carbines of various makes—lay carelessly propped against crates.

"Ladies and gentlemen," said Levitski, proudly spreading his arms. "Welcome to the revolution!"

Chapter Fourteen

The kingdom under the streets

November 28th, 1863

With the coming of dawn, discussion in the kitchens turned to how the king might get word of Jayavarthon's treachery and of his own survival to the city, in the hope of rallying loyalists to his banner. At least that was the gist of the conversation as far as I could make out.

I became aware of each member of the king's following turning their eyes upon me, one by one. Apparently I was expected to play some part in the plan. I was given a letter, hastily scribbled down and inked with some insignia which I took to be the king's seal. Many instructions accompanied this, and I grew to understand that I was being sent on a mission to deliver this letter to somebody of importance in the city. I could see that I was their last resort, as I am no fighting man and every available sword arm was required to defend the king. There was nobody left but me.

I desperately tried to get some clear directions from them but all I could learn was that the house was in the eastern quarter of the city, and a noble one. But delivering the letter was one thing. Escaping the palace without detection was another.

This was not a concern to my comrades, for they knew of a way to get me out. I was led to a window that opened onto a pagoda, and three men formed something of a human pyramid before me. Through a combination of pushing and hauling I was carried up onto a sloping terracotta roof from which I could then scramble higher and higher, like Jack climbing the giant's stairs until I was on the very top of the palace.

I have no head for heights and so my search for a way down began in earnest. The palace walls were too far to jump to, but for one section which was touched by the branches of a large cassia fistula. I made for the branches of that tree and scrambled into it like a schoolboy scrumping. The branches bent alarmingly beneath me as I climbed further and further out towards the wall, but at last I was able to get hold of it and haul myself over.

The city was a labyrinth before me; a maze of bamboo huts, muddy streets and alleys that climbed up the mountainsides. I headed east per my directions and looked for the largest of the houses there. It stood on poles above the foliage and was colourfully painted, with tall gables making it look a probable haunt for a nobleman in this country.

I knocked on the door and caused great outrage amongst the household's servants. Some wanted to force me off the property with pikes while others wanted to confine me inside for the disposal of their master. All I could do was uselessly wave the king's letter in their faces.

It was snatched from me by an elderly servant who seemed to have some authority among them. He read it thoughtfully and carried it away to his master. The next few hours were confusing and difficult to relate. My part was one of waiting. People came and went from the property and there was a great marshalling of armed men in the gardens. I breathed easy when I saw the glittering pikes and knew that my mission had been a success.

We set out as the morning broke over the golden spires of the temple; a rag-tag army of many banners. My host had called in every friend who shared his loyalty to the king, and there was much shaking of spears and chants of war.

A few arrows sang out from the walls of the palace, but most of Jayavarthon's men were still occupied with the king's forces within and we took the walls without casualties. Parties were sent out to find timber to bring down the doors and I, hoping to make myself useful in the siege, went around to the animal cages at the back in my search for something that might be used as a ram.

An elephant was being led away from the enclosures towards the eastern gate which, like all but the main gate to the palace, was devoid of guards. I recognised it at once as the trusty beast that had carried me to this lost world in the Isan mountains, and the man who led it was none other than Kasemchai.

"Where the devil are you off to?" I exclaimed, approaching him. "I thought you had been killed!"

He turned, startled and looked sheepish in the extreme. "I leave," he said. "Not safe here. You come with me?"

"But where have you been?" I asked again, not liking his evasion.

"You should not have helped king. You made matters worse. Nobody wanted war. Now, fighting in palace and revolution soon in city. I must leave."

"It was you who slipped the strychnine tree petals into the kitchens, wasn't it?" I said.

It took him a long time to reply. "No," he said. "I just deliver. Jayavarthon takes care of details. I just bring flowers."

I did not bother asking him why. What were these people to him but buyers for his goods? So what if one of them asked him to bring some poisonous flowers? It was nothing to him what they were used for. He was just a merchant. I suspected that it was also Kasemchai who alerted Jayavarthon of our ruse to draw him out. That was the bigger treachery, not least because it had put my own life in danger. I could no longer trust the guide who had brought me here. But then, how was I to return to Bangkok?

"Do not try to stop me," Kasemchai said. "I like you. Do not try..."

I could see the hilt of the long knife protruding from his breeches. I could have called for my loyalist friends. I could have made sure that Kasemchai faced justice for what he had done. But I had no wish to see him beheaded or subjected to whatever form of execution they used for traitors in this city. I have seen too much bloodshed in the last twenty-four hours that I have no stomach for any more useless killing.

I let him go.

By the time I returned to the main gate, I found it broken in and the battle had been carried into the palace without me. I wandered through the rooms as a ghost, witnessing the wreckage around me. Bodies littered the corridors. The throne room was awash with slaughter, and standing atop a mound of corpses was King Harshavarman, his face a bloody mask of victory. In his fist he held the decapitated head of Jayavarthon by the hair, while his followers chanted his name ecstatically. It was over.

I am far too tired to continue writing now and my hand aches. I shall write more tomorrow.

Lazarus and his companions were taken through a series of chambers which were filled with people at workbenches. The first was occupied primarily by women who stitched cloth by hand or beavered away at ancient Singer sewing machines. They were making uniforms; grey with red insignias. Small mountains of finished garments were piled up at the ends of the benches, and occasionally a small child of about nine or ten would come along with a little wheelbarrow, scoop up the clothes and trundle them off to some other part of the complex.

"You have children down here too?" Lazarus asked.

"Better here than on the streets above," said Levitski. "Better to join the revolution that is fighting to stop child slavery and the exploitation of our youth by the Fagins and the beadles of this fat country."

Lazarus was not convinced. The tired eyes, worn fingers and grim expressions of hopelessness on the faces of the workers they passed did not suggest that they were tasting the fruits of freedom. Revolutionist cause or no, he didn't see what was so different about this place than the sweatshops of Whitechapel.

The following room was even more alarming. There were more men at work here than in the previous room, but there was still a majority of women and it was not with needle and thread that they toiled, but with file, steel cutter and drill. Copies of well-known revolvers, rifles and carbines were in various stages of completion on the benches. Bullets were being cast, shells packed with explosives and metallic cartridges constructed.

"Munitions factory?" Lazarus asked.

"You didn't think we were fighting a war of words did you?" was Levitski's reply. He beckoned a young woman in a faded green apron over to them. "Take Ivy and Ivan here and show them their new quarters," he told her. "Meals are three times a day. On the house, naturally."

"How do you feed this army?" Lazarus asked him as the two were taken away from the group.

"Self-sufficiency mostly. We have our own bakery down here, and carriages of grain come in daily. Meat and dairy is a little harder to get, but we take what we can from the world above by whatever means necessary."

"You mean thievery?"

"Are not the true thieves the masters of the slaughterhouses and the dairies? The ones who grow fat on the toil of others? We do not steal, we merely redistribute the world's produce to those who need it."

Lazarus and Mr. Clumps were led past a series of offices partitioned off by sets of small and grubby window panes. Through the glass, Lazarus could see people hunched over drawing boards by the light of dim gas lamps. Blueprints, maps and designs plastered every available wall space. This revolution, it seemed, involved a good deal of paperwork.

"We have designers working around the clock to perfect engines of war that will shake London to its foundations," Levitski explained. "Literally."

At last, they finished up in a large office set out with tattered armchairs that looked as if they had been pillaged from an abandoned gentleman's club in the world above. A man in a frockcoat stood by a fireplace in which a mound of coals glowed. He was tall and gaunt, with a black moustache that he had waxed and curled. He had been speaking to two other men in greasy overalls and low caps. One had a spanner protruding from his pocket. Upon seeing the newcomers, he dismissed the men and they left.

"Welcome to our little republic beneath the heel of capitalism," said the man in the frock coat, in a heavy accent Lazarus instantly recognized as Russian. "I am Dr. Alexander Pedachenko."

"How do you do, doctor?" said Lazarus. "Are you in charge of this underground society?"

"We do not have rulers in the way that society upstairs do, but yes, I suppose that if anybody takes the responsibility of making sure all runs smoothly around here, then that man is me. I understand you both have army training."

"Actually only I do. But my friend here lets his size and strength speak more than any military training would."

"Yes, he is a magnificent specimen, isn't he?" Pedachenko said, looking Mr. Clumps up and down with almost perverse fascination. "Phossy jaw, I'm told? Nasty... But the mask only adds to your intimidation, comrade. It's rather spectacular, I must say. And you, comrade? Where have you served?"

"The Soudan," Lazarus replied.

"Excellent. Do you have any experience in training recruits?"

"Some. We had to train up a batch of Egyptian reserves. I was put in charge of a company."

"Good, good. Desert fighting is a lot like street fighting, I imagine. One must sometimes blend in with the surroundings and then strike from the shadows as a viper striking from the sand."

"As you say."

"Comrade, I want to put you in charge of training some of my own companies."

Lazarus stifled a smile. Pedachenko, for all his talk of a leaderless republic, had just betrayed himself by referring to the companies as 'his'. This was no socialist.

"We have no shortage of men, but they are in dire need of steering and discipline, not to mention experience."

"I'll do my best," said Lazarus, "but forgive me for asking, what is the aim of all of this?"

Dr. Pedachenko blinked. "Comrade Levitski did not tell you?"

"Oh, I understand about the overthrow of the thieving class and the rise of the proletariat and all that, but I'm just wondering how? And when? And how you, a Russian doctor of all things, came to be in charge of it? There seems to be an awful lot of Russians involved. Not to mention Jews."

"Russians, Englishmen, Jews, Christians, what is the difference when all are under the heel of the corrupt and greedy state? We have all suffered, and through our suffering we have become united in a single cause. Anarchism transcends race, religion, nationality and creed. We are not foreign conquerors but home-grown liberators! The concept of nationality is an outdated one and patriotism is the true cause of all wars. Our aim is to destroy all that is and start from Year Zero. To rebuild everything from the bottom up! To do this we shall return control of this city to its people! And with the fall of London comes the fall of Britain, then its empire and then the world!"

"Well, we're dealing with a megalomaniac," Lazarus said to Mr. Clumps once they were in the privacy of their quarters; a pair of army cots in a secluded brick archway. "For all his talk of the proletariat and democracy, he's set himself up as a Caesar down here—a Napoleon of the Mole Kingdom. Did you see poor Ivy in there, sewing away at her bench as if she never left that sweatshop on Goulston Street?"

"And Ivan is in the gun shop putting together weapons for this illegal army," Mr. Clumps said.

"With armed guards at all the exits, those poor souls are more slaves than they ever were in the world above."

"And we are just as imprisoned as they are."

"That's true."

"So what's the plan?"

"Well, I need to get word of this lunatic sect to Whitehall before that madman's plans for bloody revolution are put into place. But short of fighting our way out in a blaze of glory, I think we're stuck here for the moment. We're going to have to play along and appear to train this little army of his to his satisfaction. I'm not mad keen on the idea of preparing troops for the overthrow of the British Empire, but maybe we can learn some useful Intel that might help the authorities defeat them. Numbers, equipment, that sort of thing."

After breakfast on the following day, they were taken to a wide area in the complex that appeared to have been some sort of underground goods yard. Lines showed in the ground where the tracks had been ripped up. A regiment of troops was going through drill in their uniforms of grey and red. Several mannequins of sand-filled sacks were strung up on a petty gallows for the men to practice their bayoneting.

The drill instructor was a broad-shouldered man with a thick moustache. By his brisk way of talking, Lazarus could tell that he had been in the military—though what misdemeanor had seen him drummed out of the army and into the laboring world from which he had been plucked, Lazarus could not guess.

"You're the new drill instructor, eh?" the man said, shaking Lazarus's hand. His eyes fell on Mr. Clumps. "I say, he's a big 'un! He an instructor too?"

"Of sorts," Lazarus said. "He's mainly here as my assistant."

"Right-o. Well, as you can see, the lads are getting fairly good with the old bayonet. I've been teaching them how to do horses too, although we don't really have weapons long enough for it, of course. So, tell me about your service years. Soudan wasn't it?"

Lazarus spent the afternoon making up lies about his heroics against the followers of the Mahdi and going through drills with his new troops. Their training may have left much to be desired, but he was surprised by the quantity and quality of their equipment. As well as the rifles and carbines churned out by the gun shop, there were pikes, demolition kits and barbed anti-cavalry obstacles known as *Cheval de frise*. But most alarming of all were the armored vehicles dreamed up by Pedachenko's engineers.

They were kept in a storeroom that lay on the other side of a culvert spanned by an iron bridge. Lazarus commented on the gushing water that rushed beneath them as they crossed it to view the war machines.

"That's where we get our fresh water from," said the drill instructor. "Clean as rain. It comes into the city from the reservoirs, and is carried through culverts to the pump works and city reservoirs before being dispersed among the populace. We just get to help ourselves directly from the source. If you want an example of the proletariat taking what's owed them by bypassing the capitalist masters, look no further than this culvert."

Many of the war machines were still being worked on with spanner and welding iron. Lazarus recognized the two men they had seen in Pedachenko's office among the mechanics. The machines were the size of Brougham carriages and entirely plated in iron. Instead of wheels, they had bands of continuous track on either side, fashioned from metal segments. A narrow slit in the fore served as a window for the driver and a capsule on top seated a gunner who would control the twelve-pounder gun.

"Great, ain't they?" Lazarus's guide said. "Nothing

like them this side of the Atlantic. The designs are based on stuff used by the Americans, but the Doc's designers have put their own spin on them. Fantastic articulation. The gunner can turn his turret around three-hundred-and-sixty degrees and hit just about anything. And they're fast too, not to mention agile. They can rumble over barricades and damn-near plough through buildings. With these in our army, we'll be invincible!"

Lazarus thought that a bold claim, but he had to admit his worry for the British Army should they have to go up against these mechanical monsters.

It was a little after noon. Lazarus was beginning to wonder when the lunch hour was and what sort of food might be served to officers and troops, when a message came down from headquarters that he and Mr. Clumps were to report to the Doc immediately.

As soon as they entered his office Lazarus knew that the game was up. Sitting on a chair, her hands bound and her eyes defiant through the barest dampness of tears, was Mary Kelly. Levitski stood by, his face severe with either anger or embarrassment. A revolver was in his right hand.

"I always knew that the government would try to penetrate our security down here," Dr. Pedachenko began. "I knew that they would use common laborers posing as socialists, but I must admit, I didn't imagine that they would employ whores as their go-betweens."

Lazarus didn't try to deny he knew the girl. Levitski had seen her leaving their lodgings on the morning of the riots. He could only direct his anger at Mary for getting involved in all of this. "What the devil are you doing here?" he demanded of her.

Levitski answered for her. "I found her snooping

around outside our house in Winthrop Street."

"How did you know about that?" Lazarus asked Mary.

"I followed you," she said, keeping her voice slow and steady. It was clear she was frightened but she seemed angry too, angry at him. "I knew there was something rotten about you."

"Mary, all this, this isn't what you think. I'm not..."

"No, I'm afraid it is worse than you think, my dear," interrupted Pedachenko. "This man is an agent for either the police or the government. He has deceived you and you have become yet another victim of the state's lies. He has been using you, as they use all of us, to his advantage. I don't know if he told you if he is an anarchist, a socialist or a revolutionary, but he is, I am afraid, a spy."

"I know," Mary mumbled. "I wasn't talking..."

But Pedachenko cut her off. "These people have infiltrated us, Levitski, and you were the one who brought them here."

Levitski was visibly sweating. "*Komrad*, I..."

"Don't worry. You are too valuable as a procurer to be disposed of just yet. And everybody slips up sometimes. This is not a problem that does not have a solution. Fetch some men and take these two away. You know where."

Relieved, Levitski moved to the door and poked his head out, calling to someone in the corridor.

"And what of the girl?" Lazarus asked Pedachenko.

"She stays with me," the doctor replied with a smile. "Her crime is not yours and so neither shall her fate be."

Two burly soldiers entered the office and stood either side of them. As they seized Lazarus by the elbows, Mr. Clumps lumbered forward and sent one of them tumbling across the room. The other cocked his rifle and Lazarus cried out, "No, Clumps! Now is not the time!"

He did not doubt the big lug's willingness to clear the room and smear the walls with the blood of Pedachenko and his cronies but there had to be a smarter way. He still had his Bulldog revolver in his breast pocket, but he didn't want Mary to be caught in the crossfire. There would be another chance. There had to be.

Mr. Clumps allowed the revolutionary behind him to pound him over the back of the head with the stock of his rifle. When that did not have the desired effect of felling him, the soldiers seized him by the collar and pulled him from the room. The mechanical was entirely biddable, rendered meek by Lazarus's wishes.

Levitski pointed his revolver at Lazarus. "Come on, *class-traitor*. Let's be off."

They wound their way out of the office complex and down onto the tracks, which they followed for some time. In the enveloping darkness, Lazarus tried to think of some way of breaking free, but before any plan could be drawn up in the interior of his gradually panicking brain, they emerged into a storage yard lit by shafts of daylight that seeped in from vents in the roof.

The stench in the place was awful. Detritus was littered about, and as Lazarus inspected it he could make out bones, rags, clumps of matted hair and skulls. This was the killing fields; Pedachenko's refuse pile for all the unwanted or troublesome members of his revolution.

"Kneel," Levitski said, jamming the barrel of his pistol into the small of Lazarus's back.

"No," said Mr. Clumps. "Me first."

"As you wish, the Russian said.

Lazarus watched, helpless as the big man knelt down on the gravel, his massive arms still raised. One of the soldiers lifted his rifle and took aim at the spot on the back of Mr. Clumps's head where the hair showed between the steel mask and the brim of his hat.

"I'm going to hang that mask of yours on my bedroom wall," Levitski said with a smirk. "Once I've washed the blood off of course, and taken a good hard look at that rotted face of yours. I've been wondering what that looks like."

The chamber resounded with the deafening shot but the bullet ricocheted upwards, scoring a deep, bloody line in the back of Mr. Clump's skull. He rose.

Levitski and his soldiers gaped in disbelief. The one who had fired desperately tried to chamber another round, and the second soldier lifted his own rifle. Lazarus saw his opportunity and seized it.

With Levitski distracted by what was unfolding, Lazarus was able to move out of the line of his gun. He quickly brought his own revolver to his palm and aimed it at the second soldier. The bullet left its barrel just as Mr. Clumps swung around, balling his fist as he turned. It struck his target in the temple as Mr. Clump's meaty fist connected with his would-be executioner's jaw. It was no light tap this time. The force of the blow caved the man's teeth and jaw in and lifted him off his feet.

His body and the body of his comrade, shot through the head by Lazarus, hit the ground almost simultaneously. Levitski gibbered with fright at this sudden turning of the tables and fumbled with his revolver, firing off two shots, both going wide. In a panic he took off back down the tunnel, leaving Lazarus and Mr. Clumps in the chamber of death that smelled no sweeter for the fresh blood that now spattered its gravel floor.

Chapter Fifteen

In which our heroes return to the world above

November 29th, 1863

The palace is swept by a feeling of fresh air as after a humid storm or the first scent of spring after the snows have melted. The bodies and blood have been cleared and the gates are under repair. There is to be a great celebration tonight in honour of the loyalist victory and of those who died to achieve it.

I was shown to my new quarters this afternoon and it is here that I write as dusk touches the rooftops of the city below me. I will not have time to write more this evening. I am to be honoured as well in the celebrations tonight, and my Siamese regalia is laid out on the bed ready for me to put on. The king himself granted me this estate in the city as his thanks for my help in defending his throne. It is a large place with several rooms already filled with furniture of fine craftsmanship. The house looks out over the thatched roofs of the bamboo huts below, framed by the peaks of the mountains.

I have servants too; men and women I have not the slightest idea what to do with, especially as we do not understand each other. Further gifts from the king have made me a man rich beyond my dreams; clothes of fine silk, chests of rubies and gold and enameled charms studded with diamonds, gilded statues of Hindoo gods, gold plate and other treasures. This wealth and estate surely mean that I have been given some noble rank by the king.

It is more than I could ever hope for in a lifetime. And yet, how can I remain here? Sarah and Michael await me in Bangkok. I cannot desert them for a life of luxury here. Besides, I do not speak the language and my noble rank will surely entail some sort of duty to my king, which I would rather avoid. I must return and yet I do not know how. I have not a hope of finding my way across Isan towards the coast without help, but who among my new friends will guide me when I am now a vassal of their king?

If only I could bring Sarah and Michael back here, we might live out our days in a far more comfortable fashion than we could ever hope to back in England. But how to explain to my king that I wish to take a leave of absence so soon after his most generous gifts?

So many problems and so many possible answers! I have not time to write more. I must prepare myself for his Majesty's celebrations. All I know for now is that I must remain here for a time and try to learn the language, so that I may explain my predicament and hope to gain the king's sympathy.

<Here ends the journal>

"If we head down the tunnel in the opposite direction we should find some way out," said Mr. Clumps.

"Undoubtedly," Lazarus agreed. "But we're not leaving without Mary."

"That is very unwise."

"I don't care," Lazarus replied irritably. Mary had got herself into this mess by her own meddling but he could not leave her in Pedachenko's clutches.

"She is not essential to the mission," Mr. Clumps

stated.

"Then you head off on your own if the blasted mission is all you care about!"

"No. My orders are to protect you. Where you go, I go."

"Then come on!"

As they jogged down the tunnel back towards the complex, Lazarus knew they were heading into danger so great that it may be considered suicide but he didn't care.

"Are you in love with her?" Mr. Clumps asked, barely out of breath.

"No! Why do you ask?"

"This sort of irrational behavior indicates an infatuation with her that overrides your sense of logic."

"Overrides my...? Let's get one thing straight, Clumps. I am not you. I don't run on a furnace and cogs. I'm a human being with human feelings of empathy and compassion. I haven't got a mechanical heart."

"Actually, my heart is..."

"Oh, come on!"

They scrambled up onto the platform and instantly found themselves under fire from the guards who were watching the exits. Lazarus flung himself against the brickwork as bullets chipped off chunks of the platform. Mr. Clumps stood stock still and let several shots tear holes through his clothes and flesh while he drew his Webley.

Two guards fell dead in a matter of seconds and a third hightailed it into the complex, crying out the alarm. Mr. Clumps holstered his smoking gun.

"You'll stick out like a sore thumb if you come in with me," Lazarus told him. "Stay here and keep the exit open. I don't want to have to fight our way through a company of men on our way out."

Lazarus removed his cap and jacket and ruffled his hair before heading towards the gun shop. Soldiers pounded along the walkways above him towards the exit, and he heard Mr. Clump's Webley speak out several times. A worker wearing a red velvet navvy jacket stood with his back to him, working hard at his bench. Lazarus tapped him on the shoulder and offered his own coat, plus the three shillings that was in its left pocket, in exchange for the tattered red garment. The deal was made and Lazarus slipped further into the shop, hatless and sporting a different attire.

He headed for the offices, confident that he had not been long enough in this underground kingdom for anybody to recognize his face at a glance. Some of the soldiers he had been training that morning might pose a problem, but they were surely still going through their drills on the parade ground.

He arrived at Pedachenko's office and hugged the wall. By peering in through the window he could see that the office was empty. Where had he taken Mary?

He crept towards the corner, his fingertips brushing the wall. He nearly leapt out of his skin when his hand touched bunches of what felt like curly hair and he drew his revolver instinctively.

"I thought you had been executed!" Mary said in a voice that held a twinge of relief.

"We persuaded them to give us a stay of execution," Lazarus told her. "What on earth are you doing crawling around here on your hands and knees?"

"Trying to stay out of view of those windows! Get down before you get us both shot!"

"They won't know me from any other worker in this place. Unless I run into Pedachenko or Levitski."

"All right for some. I don't think I could pass for a rundown seamstress even if I did pinch mesself a new coat and bonnet."

"How did you get away from Pedachenko?"

"Gave him a nasty sting!" she held up a bloodied penknife triumphantly. "Always carry one after that business with the High-Rips. He was trying some of his brain-mangling nonsense on me and was so caught up in his own babble that he didn't see me cut my ropes until it was too late."

"Brain-mangling?"

"He's a hypnotist like Miss Buki. He's got half the soldiers here under his spell. Makes sense, really. I can't imagine why anybody would stay in this dump unless their brains were scrambled."

"Good God, do you think he was involved in whatever happened to Mansfield?"

"Lord knows. If he wasn't, then hypnotism is a trend that has really taken off in London."

"Did you kill him?"

"Wish I bloody did. I stuck him in the shoulder and while he was moaning and shrieking I got away. I hid around the corner and watched him stagger off to summon his cronies. Thought it best to stay put until the way was clear. To be honest, I didn't have much of a plan beyond that."

"We'll get out together. Clumps is holding the door open for us. We only have to get through the workshops without being seen."

"Easier said than done. By the way, did you come back just for me?"

"I did."

"Well, that's gentlemanly, I must say, but you're still a filthy liar."

"Look, I'm sorry I didn't tell you about all this, but it really wasn't your business. I didn't want you caught up in it..."

"I don't mean all *this*. I always knew you were a copper. I'm talking about you letting your friend—the Ripper—go scot-free."

"I don't follow you."

"When I left your place that day I gave you the bottle of ointment, I tried to get home but got caught up in the mob. I stuck with them for a time—strength in numbers—that sort of thing, but when they started looting shops I took to my heels. That got me in worse trouble; a girl on her own, 'specially one in my profession. A gang of men chased me and nearly got hold of me, but I doubled back for your place.

"When I got there I saw you two leaving with that... that *monster*, with no chains on him! I saw you get him into a cab and take him up west! I couldn't believe my eyes! After all your promises of doing your best to keep me and other girls safe, all your claims to want to keep him contained! I knew then that you were a liar when I saw you taking him off to his jolly freedom. Where is he now? Ripping up girls in the West End? Out of sight, out of mind, is that it?"

"Mary, it's the ointment that is his stimulus. Without it there is no Hyde. No Ripper. The safest place for him is in his hotel, well away from the East End and its... well, its *ladies*."

"The safest place for him is Colney Hatch. Or Brookwood Cemetery."

"I don't have time to discuss the ethics of it all with you now. We need to get a move on. Put your shawl over your curls—they're your most striking feature."

"Blimey, d'you think so?" Then she remembered herself. "Don't try to flatter your way out of my bad books!"

Lazarus ignored her and they headed out onto the shop floor, conscious of the clattering of boots on the walkways above. The tailors were so concerned with their work that none noticed them slipping between their ranks. Nevertheless, they hadn't gone more than a few yards when Mary began to have serious doubts.

"We'll never make it!" she hissed. "We've still got the gun shop to get through. We'll be spotted for sure!"

"Just keep calm and don't draw attention to yourself. Keep pace with me. Don't rush."

They made it out of the garment sweatshop and into the munitions factory. They got halfway across the floor and could see the arched exits at the other end when they were rumbled.

"Halt!" bellowed a soldier on the walkway above.

The entire shop stopped what they were doing and a deathly silence fell over the room.

"Turn around!" came the command.

Cursing their bad luck, Lazarus and Mary slowly turned to face the rifles trained on them from above. A door slammed open at the rear of the chamber and Dr. Pedachenko strode out onto the walkway, clutching his shoulder. Blood seeped through his white frock coat.

"Are you still with us?" Pedachenko asked Lazarus. "Excellent. Miss Kelly can watch you die before she faces her own execution. Bring them to me!"

The soldiers began to descend the stairs, keeping their rifles trained on them. Suddenly, two shots were fired in quick succession from the direction of the exits. Two of the soldiers tumbled headlong down the steps, both struck by bullets.

The workshop erupted into a furor of screams. All eyes were on the figure of Mr. Clumps as he strode the length of the room, firing shot after shot at the men on the walkway. Answering rounds thudded into him, wholly unheeded by the mechanical. Lazarus grabbed Mary and dragged her behind a workbench.

A bullet struck Mr. Clumps in the face and the clasp that held his mask on snapped. The steel face clattered to the floor and there were further cries of alarm as those who dared peep from cover saw the half-face of livid flesh, glassy eyes and missing jaw.

"Saints preserve us!" said Mary, gaping at the mess of pipes and tubes that formed Mr. Clumps's speaking apparatus. "What is this friend of yours?"

Pedachenko's laugh rippled in the air above them. "A mechanical! My dear boy, you've brought me a mechanical! And how cleverly disguised! I had no idea they could be so inconspicuous. Mechanite powered? But of course. The real question is how and why the American governments let the British have one of their precious slaves. But it is mine now. Imagine what we could achieve with a few grams of mechanite, comrades!"

"You'll have to pry it from his lifeless shell and over my dead body, Pedachenko!" Lazarus called up.

"This is where I'm supposed to say 'as you wish' or some dime novel cliché like that," Pedachenko retorted. "But I'll go one better. Listen to me, comrades! I want all three of these intruders dead and the brave ones who do this for me will receive double food rations for two weeks and halved working hours! Put up your rifles, men."

The soldiers on the walkway fell at ease. Lazarus looked around at the workshop. Men and women were beginning to emerge from their cover, eying them. Nervous hands fingered heavy tools.

"He's got them so starved and overworked that they'd rather kill us for a few extra scraps in the mess hall than fight for their own freedom!" Lazarus told Mary. "So much for socialism. This is slave-to-the-wage pure and simple."

"Get up and get behind me," Mr. Clumps said, his voice strange now it was no longer muffled by the mask.

They fell into a tight triangular formation, each protecting the backs of the other two. Mary had only her knife, which she held out like a toasting fork. Lazarus didn't doubt her intention of sticking anybody who got too close.

"Head for the exit," said Lazarus.

They moved slowly, a wide circle of workers enveloping them like a pack of hungry wolves. Lazarus noticed several of the soldiers edging along the walkway to the stairs by the exit, hoping to cut off their escape. He fired a couple of shots at them and made them think twice.

Somebody got too close to Mr. Clumps and the mechanical fired without hesitation, killing the man instantly. The crowd fell back, unnerved.

"Now!" Lazarus yelled and they turned and fled.

It took only a heartbeat for the workers to recover their wits and give chase. Several shots rang out from the walkway but missed their targets who were quickly through the exits. Soon, the three escapees were pounding along the platforms towards the tunnel. Lazarus felled a soldier that appeared out of nowhere and leapt over his body as it slumped to the ground.

It was useless to lead a mad chase down the tunnel with fifty factory workers after their blood, but Lazarus had a better idea. "After me!" he cried, cutting left through an archway that led to the culvert and the armored vehicle hanger.

"We'll be killed!" Mary said, eyeing the water that thundered below the iron bridge. "What's to stop us from being sucked under and drowned?"

"Can't you swim?" Lazarus asked her.

She shrugged. "Dunno. Never tried. Not much call for it in Limerick, unless you go in the sea which is too cold by half."

Lazarus groaned. "Well you'll have to learn pretty sharpish or we all wait here and face the mob."

The crowd of workers was fast approaching down the corridor.

"Look, I'll hold onto you," Lazarus told her. "All you have to do is keep kicking with your feet and only take a breath when you get the chance."

"Where does all this water go, anyway?"

"Some reservoir, I expect. Or maybe directly into the Thames."

"All right then. But you hold on to me bloody tight, mister!"

"Good. Ready?"

"No," said Mr. Clumps.

"What?"

"I can't join you."

"Why ever not?"

"I'm not waterproof. My furnace would be dampened and I would sink to the bottom."

"Christ, I never thought of that! What can we do?"

"You both go. I'll fight my way down the tunnel and

we'll meet on the surface."

"All right, but I want no heroics from you, Clumps. Just push through and get to the nearest station or exit you can find. We're headed for the nearest police station. You do the same and I'll put out a telegraph for you."

"Get moving then," said the mechanical and he lumbered off back the way they had come, his pistol lighting up the brick arches with orange flashes.

Lazarus grabbed hold of Mary's hand and jumped, pulling her down with him to hit the foaming torrent below.

Chapter Sixteen

In which the revolution begins

They rose up in a flurry of bubbles and broke the surface, gasping for air. It was dark—the echoes of dripping water told Lazarus that they had emerged in one of London's underground reservoirs. Mary's dress and petticoats were sodden and she weighed a ton.

"Keep kicking!" Lazarus told her, frightened that she might pull him under.

"I'm trying!" she spluttered.

A faint light flickered across the water's surface far out in the blackness. Lazarus made for it with Mary's arms over his shoulders. It was a hard swim, but eventually his knees banged against the brick steps that led up towards the light. A vertical ladder of iron rungs led up to a barred inspection cover through which light streamed.

Lazarus put his shoulder to it, heaved it up and slid it across. They emerged, sodden and cold, in what looked like a park lit by moonlight. They wrung the water out of their clothes and stamped about in an attempt to get warm.

"I'll catch my death like this!" Mary complained.

It was no exaggeration. The October night was chill and the wind cut through their soaking garments like a knife. They had to find somewhere warm, and get into some dry clothes quickly.

"Any idea where we are?" Mary asked.

"Not a clue. Still in London, at least."

They headed over to the iron railings that fenced the park and spent some time looking for a cab. When they got one, Lazarus told the driver to take them to the nearest police station.

The sergeant at Muswell Hill Police Station eyed them skeptically as Lazarus told him that they had recently escaped from an underground (in every sense of the word) revolutionary society that intended the overthrow of the British state. He was even more skeptical when the bedraggled and dripping man on the other side of his desk claimed to be a government agent, with an urgent message for Whitehall which must be sent immediately.

It was a frustrating ten minutes as Lazarus told and retold his story, while they stood dripping wet with the sergeant frowning at what he clearly considered a raving madman and a prostitute who had recently taken a drunken plunge in the River Lea.

Eventually the message got through that they were to be taken seriously. They were given blankets, hot tea and were allowed to dry themselves by the little potbelly stove in the parlor while the sergeant saw that Lazarus's message was sent. It would go directly to Morton's office.

"My superior will have the military flush Pedachenko's revolution out of its warren, like rats from a sewer," Lazarus told Mary as they sipped their tea, steam curling up from their clothes.

She did not answer and he sensed that in her heart she still poured scorn on him.

"Look, I'm sorry about Mansfield," he said. "But I

really acted in everybody's best interests. I couldn't very well leave him in Limehouse while Clumps and I went on this jaunt with the revolutionaries."

"I don't suppose you left anybody to guard over him at his hotel?" Mary asked. "Police or anybody?"

"No, I can't allow his condition to become known. But you must trust me on this, Mary. I would never do anything that would put you or any other girl in danger. I promise."

"What's become of Mr. Clumps?"

"I mentioned him in my dispatch. They'll find him and have him sent here."

It became apparent that some sort of excitement was unfolding by the main desk. Sergeants and inspectors hurried in and out of offices with bits of paper and there was a general feeling of tense agitation.

"What's up?" Lazarus asked the sergeant at the desk.

"Sounds like your underground boys have made their first blow against us," the sergeant replied gravely. "Somebody just detonated a device in the London Stock Exchange."

"Christ almighty!"

"The wire's on fire with it. We're all being notified to watch out for any similar attacks. This sound like your Russian fellow?"

"Absolutely. There is no shortage of explosives in his lair. He must be accelerating his plans after our escape. He knows that I can lead the authorities to him and is starting his war right now!"

"Then he must be halted in his tracks," said a voice. A tall man with a dark brown side parting and a long moustache stood in the doorway, removing his hat. Lazarus recognized him as Sir Charles Warren, the

Commissioner of the Metropolitan Police. A second man with large side whiskers stood beside him. Lazarus felt he had seen him before but couldn't remember where. They both wore great coats and had just come in from the cold. "But what we need to know from you, Mr. Longman," Warren went on, "is where he will strike next."

"I can't answer that, sir," said Lazarus. "I was put in charge of training his troops for a morning, but was not privy to his master plan."

"You mean to say," broke in the bewhiskered man at Warren's side, "that you had a hand in training this army of lunatics at his command?"

"This is Inspector Frederick Abberline from Scotland Yard," said Warren. "He used to work for A Division and knows your superiors very well."

Yes, Lazarus might have seen Inspector Abberline at Whitehall but it was far more probable, he felt, that he recognized those graying whiskers from the press reports of the police's investigation into the Ripper murders. Abberline was one of the chief officials on the case.

"My involvement was minimal," Lazarus explained, "and entirely necessary to keep my cover."

"Your cover?" said Abberline with a snarl. "I don't know what orders Morton gives you fellows, but it goes against my gut to be forced to let you prance all about this city as if you were above the law. If I had my way you'd all be locked up for obstructing justice. I know all about the red tape that Morton slips you boys under, red tape the rest of us have to stick by."

"Calm yourself, Frank," said Warren. "We don't have time to vent our frustrations concerning other agencies. Now then, lad. Anything you remember that might be of any help?"

Lad? thought Lazarus with indignation. If these old fools had seen half the things he had in the pursuit of his ludicrously dangerous missions all around the world in the service of the empire, they'd be treating him with a damned sight more respect.

"It'll be a symbol of capitalism or state control," he answered at length. Then it came to him. "Greenwich Observatory!"

"What has the observatory got to do with capitalism?" Warren asked.

"When my associate and I were brought down to Pedachenko's underground lair we were met by an armed patrol who said they had been checking the exits at Greenwich and the Docklands. As the home of the Prime Meridian, Greenwich Observatory is a symbol of the status quo. Pedachenko was ranting about bringing down all that is and starting from scratch. He's gone after the economy and now he wants to attack time itself!"

"Right, sergeant," said Commissioner Warren to the man at the desk. "Wire to Greenwich Station and tell them to get every copper they have to form a perimeter around the observatory. Pay special attention to the park. Get all the night time strollers out of it. And have officers keep a watch on who comes out of Maze Hill Station. I'll be there in a tick."

"Room in your cab for two more?" Lazarus asked the Commissioner.

"Two? You're not thinking of taking this blower along, are you?" said Abberline with a glance to Mary.

"Watch who you're calling names, copper!" Mary interjected.

"Do you want to spend the night in the nick?"

Abberline said to her, his fist held threateningly under her nose.

"She comes with us," Lazarus affirmed. "The stock exchange was just the beginning. I hope you've got all your coppers to hand, Commissioner, because London is set to become a warzone within the hour. And I'm not letting this woman wander off home through it all alone. Where I go, she goes."

"For the love of Christ," Warren wheezed. "But only because there is no time to argue."

They all scrambled into the Commissioner's Clarence outside, and the driver gave the horses such a lash that they shot off down the street like a bat out of hell.

"Run many people over in your line of work, Commissioner?" Mary asked him.

Lazarus gritted his teeth. He would have to have a word with her about insolence when time permitted. But the Commissioner's face was a picture, he had to admit.

When they rolled up outside Maze Hill Railway Station they saw that the Commissioner's wire had been received. Officers in uniform stood guard at the exit, analyzing anybody and everybody who emerged through its doors. They gulped at the sight of Commissioner Warren in his silk hat and cape, sweeping towards them like a phantom.

"Have you fellows got all the entrances to the observatory bolted up tight?" he demanded.

"Yes, sir," one of them replied. "Inspector Bellamy is there himself."

"And the park is clear?"

"Um, I don't know about that sir. Inspector Bellamy said to focus all our efforts on evacuating the observatory and making sure nobody gets in."

"Damn him!" Warren cursed. "They could come at us from any side and we wouldn't know about it until they were too close."

They hurried into the park and made their way towards the observatory's northern entrance. There were still a few people wandering the nighted green under the trees like specters in the moonlight. When they got to the observatory, Commissioner Warren let rip into Inspector Bellamy about insubordination.

Lazarus felt that this was not wholly deserved. After all, the poor inspector had only a handful of men and he had been right to evacuate the building. But Warren was a man under intense pressure these days. The press did not make light of the inability of the Commissioner and the men under his command to catch the Ripper. Baseless accusations were hurled at him and it seemed that he could not win on either front. If he swamped Whitechapel with uniformed men then he was accused of being a tyrant, yet if he sent them in plainclothes, nobody noticed them and bemoaned the lack of a police presence to protect them.

Well, few will be bemoaning the lack of coppers on London's streets by the end of this night, Lazarus thought to himself grimly.

Orders were given to rid the park of all its occupants and little by little, under the stern commands and gentle prods of the constables' truncheons, people began to dissipate. But for every one that left the park, two seemed to take his place. It became apparent that the police cordon was a subject of excitement, and drew spectators from the streets surrounding the park.

"The damned fools don't know that we're trying to protect them," grumbled Inspector Abberline. He turned to Lazarus. "Why don't you nip back to the station and inform the officers there to start telling people that they're not to go into the park."

Lazarus was about to tell the inspector that he should send one of his own bloody men on his errands, when he spotted a figure in a flat cap and open jacket that had slipped by the policemen and was heading towards them. "There!" he cried. "Stop that fellow!"

Abberline called the attention of two nearby officers and told them to apprehend the man.

"No!" Lazarus snapped, noticing the container swinging in his grip. "He's carrying something."

It looked for all the world like a tin of something one might purchase in a hardware shop; varnish or paint.

"Keep away from him!" Lazarus ordered the men.

The two coppers halted in their tracks and looked back at him dumbly. Lazarus drew his revolver. "You there!" he cried out to the man with the tin. "Stand still! Don't come any further! I'm warning you! I'll shoot!"

The man, as if deaf, continued his brisk pace. Lazarus knew it was futile to try and persuade him. This was undoubtedly one of Pedachenko's mind-controlled puppets. He would waste no more time attempting to negotiate. He fired once and hoped the hit would not be fatal.

He was to be disappointed. The man stumbled and fell. As soon as the varnish tin hit the grass there was an almighty explosion. Turf was torn up and showered like confetti through a billowing cloud of smoke, in which body parts rained down with heavy thuds.

"My God," said Abberline. "What could his intention have been? There was no way he could have detonated that device and made it out alive."

"Pedachenko has hypnotized his men into suicidal followers," Lazarus said. "I suspect it was a similar story at the Stock Exchange."

"Suicide bombers," Abberline mumbled in disbelief. "What in God's name is the world coming to?"

Commissioner Warren appeared behind them. "They'll need to break out the shovels for that one," he said in a flat tone. "But we've got worse problems."

Lazarus and Abberline turned to him.

"There's a mob running riot in the East End. They're storming factories and sweatshops, beating up foremen and persuading the workers to join them."

"Have the military been called in?" Lazarus asked him. "Pedachenko's got war machines; armored things with guns."

"The 8th Hussars and the 11th Horse Artillery are on their way," Warren replied. "As well as two infantry regiments. But they won't get through for some time. I've had every available constable, life guard and volunteer marshaled at the stations on Leman Street and East India Dock Road. We're for Leman Street. On the way you can tell me more about these war machines of his."

They bundled back into the Clarence and headed north east. By the time they had reached Limehouse, the evidence of the riot was clear. Smoke from burning buildings hovered over the streets like a fug, lit from beneath by an orange glow. People were everywhere; most were frightened Londoners wandering about in a state of shock. Others were looters taking advantage of the situation by smashing shop windows and snatching what they could, resulting in ferocious brawls with the proprietors.

"Take us down some back streets," Commissioner Warren told the driver, poking his head out of the window. "Don't try to get through this."

The Clarence lurched to the left and wound off down a narrow side street. It wasn't long before they found their way blocked once again. A Clarence much like their own lay overturned in the street, one of its horses dead and the other broken free from its reigns and nowhere in sight. The carriage was on fire and a crowd stood around it. The two passengers lay dead in the street, their fine clothes torn and their faces bloodied.

"The bastards!" Abberline hissed, drawing his pistol.

Warren grabbed his arm. "Leave it, Frank."

"Why do this?" Abberline said, seemingly on the verge of tears.

"It's the glorious revolution," Lazarus told him. "No toff is safe now. These people have been stirred up into a frenzy for the blood of those who have lorded it over them for centuries."

"Turn around, driver!" Warren called up.

"Can't, sir!" came the reply. "Street's too narrow."

"Well back it up or something, man!"

It was too late. The crowd had spotted them. Their angry cries swept towards them like a tsunami as they surged forward, bricks, bats, clubs and knives in their hands.

"You have my permission, Inspector," said Warren, his face pale as he fumbled for his own revolver.

Lazarus drew his too and as one they opened the doors of the carriage and leaned out, firing into the crowd. Several of the rioters fell dead and Warren yelled to the driver to plough through them.

The carriage trundled forward, and the terrified horses reared up at the faces of the crowd that pressed close. The driver lashed them on and one rioter was crushed under the wheels of the carriage. Abberline, to his credit, thought of a plan that Lazarus wished he had. Reaching out through the window and plucking one of the lanterns from the carriage's side, the inspector hurled it at the feet of the rioters.

The explosion of flame forced the crowd back. Lazarus did the same from his window and they quickly found themselves engulfed by fire on either side. They could hear the driver's moans and feverish prayers as he pushed on, the horses eager to leave the inferno behind them.

More people pressed in from the right and crashed against the side of the carriage, pawing, clawing at its doors to get in at the occupants. Abberline fired again and again through the open window, but there weren't enough bullets between them for the entire mob.

The carriage began to tip under the press of bodies. Lazarus grabbed Mary. "Keep your head down and be ready to run when I say," he told her.

She squeezed him tight and shut her eyes in terror as the carriage toppled. All the windows shattered as the overturned carriage struck the cobbles. The occupants were tumbled end over end in a jumble of flailing limbs. Then the crowd was upon them.

Chapter Seventeen

In which London faces another Great Fire

Scrambling over the cursing Abberline, Lazarus booted open the door of the carriage and rose up as one might rise from a grave. He shot the closest rioter to him, then slammed the butt of the revolver down on the head of a man who was trying to climb up over the axle of the ruined carriage.

Warren and Abberline joined him and between the three of them they managed to hold the crowd at bay. Lazarus helped Mary up and out of the carriage and they jumped down onto the cobbles, dashing towards a row of darkened and looted shops.

Lazarus did not notice Warren and Abberline taking off in a different direction until they had ducked into an alleyway. It was deathly silent but for the muted cries of the crowd on the street behind them. None had apparently seen them slip away and for a moment, Lazarus felt a twinge of guilt and sympathy for the commissioner and the inspector, who had no doubt drawn the brunt of the crowd's attention.

"This is a bloody nightmare!" Mary said. "What are we going to do? We can't get through to Whitechapel. It's impossible!"

"Then we head for the police station in East India Dock Road," Lazarus told her. "Or, failing that, my place. It's not exactly safe, but we can lie low for a bit and hope we can hold out for the night."

They made their way east, using the narrow backstreets and alleys and avoiding Commercial Road until it became East India Dock Road. Rejoining it, they found that another mob was rampaging up and down within yards of the police station, smashing windows and stealing goods.

"Lazarus, I'm scared," Mary said, clutching him as they stood in the shadows of the alley, peeping out like spectators to the end of the world.

Lazarus was scared too. The whole city was going up in smoke, but he had to remain firm for Mary's sake. "Look how we're dressed," he told her. "A docker and a bag-tail. They won't care about us. We'll blend right in."

They moved out onto the street and followed its gutter. Up ahead, a crowd had gathered around some poor wretch like scavengers around a wounded animal. They struck at him with bats and bits of pipe, and Lazarus had to wonder how anyone could withstand such a beating. Then he recognized the tattered greatcoat encasing the massive muscles and knew why.

"It's Clumps!" he said.

"Oh, the poor thing!" Mary exclaimed, and then remembered herself and added, "does he feel pain, do you think?"

"I've often wondered that myself. Look at him stand up to them, though!"

The mechanical was not going down without a fight; that much was clear. He swung with his fists as if he were batting at flies, felling men left, right and centre. The ground was littered with the bodies of the fallen, but that only seemed to drive the mob on in their ferocity. The sight of his grotesque face with all its pipes and tubes had probably frightened them into a rage. People will always seek to destroy what they fear, Lazarus thought grimly.

There was nothing for it. Although he desperately wanted to deliver Mary safely to the police station, he could not pass by and leave his old comrade to be torn apart by his fellow Londoners. He fired into the crowd and felled a man who was swinging a crowbar at Mr. Clumps. Heads turned, including that of the mechanical.

The sight of Lazarus and the danger he had brought on himself by killing a rioter spurred Mr. Clumps to even greater brutality. Smashing the face of the nearest assailant, he ploughed forward like a great bear protecting its young. People were crushed underfoot as he came towards Lazarus, decreasing the number of hostiles even further.

Feeling less confident about beating a lone man to death when that man's comrade was opening fire on them from the rear, the crowd fell back and contented themselves by yelling "Freak!" and "Get gone, monster!"

"Glad you made it," Lazarus said to Mr. Clumps, slapping him on the back as the reunited trio took off down the street.

"Likewise," the mechanical replied in his usual calm voice. He puffed on his cigar and exhaled a vast cloud of steam. "And you, Miss Kelly."

"What the devil's been happening to you?" Lazarus asked him.

"I lost Pedachenko's men in the tunnels and caught a train headed east."

"Caught a train? Didn't your face alarm the passengers?"

"I hung on to the back of the last carriage and rode it to Stepney, where I managed to get into the police station without drawing attention to myself."

"I'll bet you gave those coppers a fright!" said Mary, with a short laugh.

"They didn't know whether to greet me or shoot me," he continued. "But your message had got through to all the stations and so I was made as welcome as best the circumstances allowed. I stuck near the telegraph operator and kept tabs on incoming messages. He didn't like that too much, but I pointed out to him that as top secret government property I probably outranked him, and he didn't have much of a choice but to be my friend for a while.

"It wasn't long before word came through that you had been at Muswell Hill Station, but had moved on to Greenwich. If you were still in the company of Commissioner Warren, then you were expected at either Leman Street or East India Dock Road within the hour. The rioting was so bad in Whitechapel that nobody could get through. The mobs and Pedachenko's soldiers have blockaded most of the streets and are engaged in fire fights with the infantry regiments as we speak. I decided to try for East India Dock Road."

"That's where we're headed," said Lazarus. "It's the only safe place nearby. We can hold out there."

"No we can't."

"What do you mean?"

"There are no policemen left at the station."

"What? Where are they all?"

"Killed. The mob succeeded in storming the station not long after I got there. It was a bloodbath. I am the only one left. They dragged me out into the street to kill me and they would have succeeded had you not come by in the nick of time. Thank you."

"Don't mention it," Lazarus replied, but his head was whirling. *The police station overrun? Every copper killed?* It was abominable.

"Where the hell do we go now?" Mary asked, desperation showing in her voice.

"North," said Lazarus. "To Edmonton."

"That's miles away! What's in Edmonton anyway?"

"My... the man who raised me. We can follow the River Lea. The mobs won't have spread to the valley and we'll be under the cover of darkness."

Mary seemed unsure. She must have been exhausted, and her boots were falling apart. But she bore herself up bravely. "All right," she said. "Let's get a move on."

They passed the police station, and had to cross the street to avoid being scorched by the inferno. Flames roared from every window. To Lazarus, it was a symbol of chaos's victory over order. How could sanity hope to survive in a world gone insane?

As they headed north they saw evidence of hard fighting between the military and the mobs. A few dead horses along with their riders—both police and Hussars—lay in the shadows cast by the streetlights, like giant slugs oozing liquid. The bodies of rioters choked some streets, strewn between smashed barricades of fruit carts and furniture, beaten and trampled by the passing of the military.

The factories at Homerton were eerily silent since the desertion of their workers. Their gates hung open onto empty yards, where goods and tools lay abandoned. They crossed the fields and descended into the Lea Valley, following the tow path north. Once they were above Hackney Marsh, they felt well out of the city and for the time being, out of trouble.

It was pitch black. The moonlight shone through the trees on their left, screening off the hell that had consumed London. The peace was enjoyable but it was not to last. They approached a public house in Tottenham which had been visited by the rioters. The door had been kicked in and its yard was in a shambles.

"Probably looking for drink to spur them on," said Lazarus.

"There's a light burning inside," said Mr. Clumps.

"Let's move on," said Mary. "No point hanging around here."

"Aren't you hungry?" Lazarus asked her.

"They won't be open at this time."

"Open? The place barely has a door."

"So you intend to steal from the proprietor like common looters?"

"Let's just see if anybody's about." He drew his pistol but let Mr. Clumps go in first. The sight of him alone should terrify any lingering looters into submission.

It was dim inside, but the light came from behind the door of a back room. Mr. Clumps slowly opened it and found himself staring down the barrel of a Martini-Henry rifle. It was held by a member of the Royal Horse Artillery.

"Bloody hell!" the soldier said at the sight of the mechanical's face. "Now I know I've gone mad!"

"At ease, soldier," Lazarus said, slowly holstering his pistol. "Don't be alarmed by my friend here. He's quite harmless. I understand your shock but he's something of a new science project the government is working on."

"Government fellows, are you?" the soldier asked. "What are you doing here, then?"

"We saw the door broken in and a light burning. Just thought we'd take a look."

"Why are you abroad at this time of night?"

"Escaping the madness in the city. We're headed for Edmonton. What happened here?"

"A bloody massacre, that's what happened. They came on this place like a swarm of Zulus, not like Englishmen at all. They were looking for drink."

"Where's the proprietor?"

"Dead. They knocked his head in before we got here."

"We?"

"Me and Tommy, here." He indicated a wounded man who was stretched out in the corner of the room, almost hidden by the shadows. Blood soaked through the bed sheets that had been used to cover him. He was watching them through half-closed eyes.

"What are you fellows doing so far out if it?" Lazarus asked, conscious that he may be dealing with deserters.

"We're all that's left! They tore us apart! You can drop us in it for deserting if you will but I'll not regret our actions. It was flee or be butchered. We're not trained for this!"

"What happened?"

"They've been storming the prisons and arming the convicts. We were sent down to Newgate to disperse the mob at its gates. It was a proper siege! They had men in uniform standing on overturned carriages giving speeches about overthrowing the old system and starting from scratch, new laws, new philosophies and that meant that all incarcerated under the old system had to be freed! We fired grapeshot and canister into the crowd and that pushed them back a bit, but they came at us with bloody war machines! Like the ones they have in America you see illustrated in the papers."

"Not quite like them," said Lazarus. "These revolutionists have no access to mechanite, thank God."

"Say what you like, mister, it made little difference to us. Those things are impenetrable! We fired everything we had at them and they kept on coming. Then they opened fire and decimated our guns and there wasn't a bleeding thing we could do about it! We fell back. It was chaos. I saw good mates of mine blown apart before my very eyes. Tommy here took a piece of shrapnel in the arm."

"Let me take a look at him," said Mary, kneeling down at Tommy's side.

"We headed north," continued the soldier. "The fires and the looting had spread ahead of us. Well to-do houses were being ransacked right in front of us and their occupants dragged out into the street. I just kept pushing on with Tommy over my shoulder, resting whenever there was a safe spot and moving on when it got too hot. We were ravenous and needed clean water, not to mention somewhere to get a bit of kip. We came upon this place just as the looters were moving on."

All throughout the soldier's story his eyes had been flitting to the half-face of Mr. Clumps. "I never seen anything like this fellow," he mumbled. "Are you all from the government?"

"I and my friend are, but Mary here is just somebody we picked up. A friend."

"Got any water?" Mary asked. "His wound wants washing."

"Got some here," the soldier said, handing her his canteen. "I was gonna get around to doing it myself but I heard you lot approaching. Besides, he's the better for a woman's touch. You a nurse?"

"Do I look like one?" she replied. "But I've patched up enough cuts and scrapes in my time. He'll need a doctor's attention, but I think I can fix him up enough so's he's likely to survive the night."

"Much obliged, miss," the soldier said.

"Got any gin?"

Lazarus fetched her half a bottle from the next room that had survived the mob and handed it to her. "I thought you were against the idea of looting."

"It's for disinfecting the wound," she said, giving him a withering look. She uncorked it with her teeth and took a long swig. "Anyway, the proprietor is dead so it's not really thieving."

Lazarus sent Mr. Clumps to scavenge what he could from the larder while he helped himself to some weak ale in the bar. The mob had left little, but there was some dried sausage to be had, some cheese and a few old biscuits. They shared their feast with the soldiers and enjoyed the brief respite.

"What's the plan, then?" Mary asked Lazarus. "Stop the night here? There's food and drink and an extra man to stand watch."

"No," Lazarus replied. "We've come this far. I want to go on. Edmonton isn't far now."

"I'm sure your old man can wait for the morning."

"I'm not so sure. He's not well, you see, and I have been lax in my duties as a son of late. With the city going up in smoke and brother turning on brother, it's got me thinking of him and I can't stop now. Not when we're so close. I need to see that he's all right."

Mary accepted this and, loath to be up on their feet again and leaving the safety of the public house, they said their farewells to the soldiers and wished them all the luck that was to be had in a world turned upside-down.

"Thank you for understanding," Lazarus told Mary after they had walked the first mile in silence.

"Don't mention it," she replied. "I never really saw eye to eye with me own da. But I was sorry when he died. It happened a few years ago. I was in London and hadn't paid him a thought for many months. When I heard that he was dead I wished I had. He was all right, really. Not a drunk or a beater and he kept us fed. I suppose that's about as much as anyone can ask for."

"Yes," said Lazarus. "I suppose it is."

Chapter Eighteen

In which a second night is had at the theatre

When they got to Edmonton the sky in the east was a purplish blue, dawning on a changed England. The fires of London underlit the thick fug of acrid smoke that hung over the city like a pall. Whatever this new day would bring, Lazarus thought, it had to be an improvement on the previous one.

Alfred's condition was worse than he expected. He was wracked with coughs and his blanket was smeared with blood. It didn't look like he had been up and about anytime recently.

"Hasn't the doctor come by?" Lazarus asked him.

"Fat chance," he replied. "From what you've been telling me the whole city has gone to pot. Maybe the whole country, too."

"I'm sure the military will have things sorted out in a day or two."

Alfred sneered and coughed some more. Mary heated up water for him on the stove, while Mr. Clumps sat by the window peering out at the gradually lightening street, still on guard as if he could never be anything but on duty.

They made some tea and Lazarus fed Alfred some. Mary took a liking to the old man and pandered to him, cleaning his face with a warm cloth and fetching fresh sheets from a cupboard on the landing.

"Nice girl, you've found there," Alfred told Lazarus when she was gone. "Think you might let her make an honest man of you?"

"Mary? Oh, we're not... it's not... I just met her while on the job. She's only tagging along because I didn't want her wandering around London with all this rioting."

"You seem rather concerned for her safety if she's just someone you met 'on the job'."

"Just trying to be a gentleman."

"You know you're not all that bad," Albert said with a smile that bordered on sympathy. "She might be very grateful for your chivalry. Women have married men for less..."

"Marriage? You don't understand. She's... well... she's a..."

"I'm well aware of what she is, son. I'm old and dying but I'm not blind. I'm a man of the world. You might make honest people of each other."

"I don't think so."

"I'm not going to be one of those interfering old people and say that you can't stay a bachelor forever. I'm the living proof that one can. I just don't want you to end up like me. I want you to have what I never had. A wife and children of your own. That would be just the thing to pull you out of this business with the government. It would be a chance for a normal life."

"What's a normal life these days when London itself is going up in smoke?" Lazarus asked.

Alfred was quiet at this. Then he said; "You wouldn't even have to stay in England. She might be persuaded to go abroad with you."

"I thought you said you wanted me out of the

government's employ."

"You'll find your own way, as I did. You never know what employment you might find in the big wide world, or whom you might pick up on the way."

"A scruffy little pickpocket to call my own?"

Alfred managed a weak cackle which nearly set him off on one of his coughing fits. "Have you given any thought to finding out what happened to your real father?" he wheezed.

"Not really."

"There may be a fortune awaiting you. Constantine Westcott seems to think so. It might be worth pursuing. Besides, you don't know that your father is even dead. He could still be there, living like a prince in clothes of silk and gold."

"If he is, then he's a cad of the highest order," said Lazarus with a touch of poison in his voice. "He left my mother and I in Bangkok and never returned for us. I just hope he is dead so that I may think something of him, at least. Besides, he is not my true father."

Albert's eyes studied him intently, wetness showing at the corners. Lazarus patted his hand. "My true father is right here in London."

They slept until ten o'clock; until the low autumn sunlight shone in between the curtains and woke them. When they rose, they found that Albert Longman had died in the night.

"Lazarus, I'm so sorry," Mary said, touching his shoulder.

Lazarus was sorry too. Sorry that he hadn't been able to get Albert into a good hospital. Sorry that he hadn't been able to spend more time with him in his last days. Sorry that he had not been the son he should have been.

"Let's head back towards the city," he said. "I'll make funeral arrangements as soon as I am able. Things might have quietened down a bit."

"What if they haven't?" Mary said. "What if Pedachenko is in control of the city and England is lost?"

"Then we'll have to build new lives somewhere else," he said. "All three of us."

As it turned out, the world hadn't ended. As they entered the city they saw signs of people trying to piece together their lives. Many walked about in a daze as if the events of the previous night were some sort of horrible dream. But the wreckage that lay all about was proof that it wasn't. Shopkeepers prized off the wooden boards from their windows and tried to reorganize what was left of their stock. Corpses were cleared from the streets and piled up in neat rows, as if they were rubble.

By questioning a series of people they encountered, they received a fragmentary account of what had happened. After the defeat of the 11th Horse Artillery outside Newgate Prison, a general retreat had been called. Marshalling their forces west of Regent Street, the military had awaited reinforcements in the form of the 3rd Durham Volunteer Artillery. Once they had arrived, they had been able to smash the revolution's armored vehicles with a combination of Howitzers and Maxim Guns. Large areas of Soho and Covent Garden were rubble now, but they had hammered the mobs into submission.

Then came the dangerous task of ridding the underground of the remnants of Pedachenko's army. Infantry regiments marched down the tracks at Maze Hill, Blackfriars and the old Whitechapel station.

Reports came to the surface that little resistance was met, nearly all of the revolution's soldiers having been killed in the battle above. The majority of the wretches down there were worn out workers who wanted nothing more than to see daylight again.

It was over and, while reeling from the blow that it had been struck, London would stagger to its feet and carry on as it had always done throughout history.

"Looks like we can finally go home," said Mary as they approached the East End.

"Can we walk you to Miller's Court?" Lazarus asked her. "I'd feel a lot better if you'd let us."

She smiled. "All right. But then I'd best be seeing about getting back to work tonight. I imagine most men in Whitechapel are in need of a good fuck to take their mind off things. Unwind a little. I might make a fortune!"

Lazarus did not laugh. He was still thinking about his father's parting words to him. Could he make it work with a girl like Mary? Could he make an honest woman out of her? Or her a decent man out of him?

"No sign of this Pedachenko fellow," said Morton when Lazarus—bathed, trimmed and in a new suit—sat before his desk that afternoon. "Seems to have given us the slip, although we have all ports on alert for a man fitting his description. He'll be trying to make his way back to Russia."

"How can you be so sure?" Lazarus asked.

"I've had our agents over there do some digging. Alexander Pedackenko is something of a chameleon. He sometimes goes by the name of Count Luiskovo."

"Count? That doesn't sound like much of an anarchist."

"Well no, that's the interesting bit. All our sources seem to suggest that he is not an enemy of the Tsarist regime at all. There was nothing that forced him to leave Russia and seek amnesty on our shores. Unless, of course, it was his orders from the Okhrana."

"The Okhrana?" exclaimed Lazarus, astonished.

"Looks like our revolutionary leader was nothing more than an agent provocateur sent by the Russian secret police to stir up trouble here in London. I'd say he went above and beyond in the call of duty."

"The whole thing was a sham? But the violence.... the lives lost..."

"Such are the morals of our opponents in this tournament of shadows we play," Morton replied with a grim smile. "The lives of pawns cost little and there are so very many of them."

"But the revolution very nearly succeeded. Would Russia really have wanted an anarchist state setting the example for the rest of Europe?"

"I imagine they were as surprised by the level of Pedachenko's success as we were. I think their aim was to cause as much havoc in London as possible and, should the unthinkable happen—the downfall of the British Empire—whatever rose from its ashes would be green and young and easily crushed under their boot."

Lazarus was silent. He was shocked at how casually the great powers in the world threw away human lives as if people were mere logs to be cast on the furnace of a steam engine, driving it ever onwards.

"Well, despite half the city being in ruins," Morton went on, "I think we can say that your mission was a resounding success. Well done, old chap. I knew you could pull it off. And just in time, too. I would hate to think what would have happened had all this revolution malarkey gone off when Bismarck was in the thick of London society."

Lazarus blinked. He had forgotten about Bismarck's impending visit.

"I imagine Pedachenko would not have let a chance to pick off his master's great enemy slip by. That would have been catastrophic for our relations with Prussia."

"When is Bismarck getting here?" Lazarus asked.

"Arriving in three days. The Prussian officials tried to call off the visit when they heard what was happening in London, but their chancellor convinced them to postpone it for only a few days. That old warhorse won't let a petty revolution stand in the way of his plans for Europe. I'm to be part of the host delegation unfortunately. I loathe social functions. We're going to the theatre of all things to see that blasted Jekyll and Hyde play. I'm dreading it."

"Jekyll and Hyde..." mumbled Lazarus, not sure if he had heard him correctly.

"Yes, apparently the PM thinks it's important to give our Prussian friend the full English experience. Although what a play written by a Scotsman and acted out by Americans says about English culture, I daren't say."

As the patrons filed in from the lobby to find their seats, Lazarus felt as if he had stepped back in time, as if the past few months had only been a dream. Part of him wanted to enjoy the illusion. He forced himself to remember all that had happened, and that he was here to convince his friend to stop performing and seek the help he needed.

It was madness for Mansfield to walk onstage in front of an audience culled from all over London. His hotel rooms were the only safe place for him. It was not likely that any East End bag-tail would be in the audience reeking of the stuff that drove Mansfield to murder, but Lazarus felt uncomfortable all the same. He understood that Mansfield lived to perform, that he was nothing if he was not onstage and that the production's recent hiatus must have felt like some kind of exile for him, but it was too soon, too dangerous.

His psychological problems had to be addressed before he could return to public life. As soon as the performance was over, Lazarus would confront him in his room and arrange a meeting with Miss Buki. He would have to bring the gypsy to him. It was too risky to take Mansfield into the East End. Well, so be it. He would do whatever it took to root out the worm that was slowly eating its way through the core of Mansfield's mind.

In the boxes opposite, he could see some familiar faces in the delegation taking their seats. Morton was there, as was the PM. Several men in Prussian uniforms indicated the presence of the visiting dignitary, and the balding fellow with the white caterpillar under his nose could only be Bismarck himself.

The atmosphere was tense. Other audience members gazed up at the boxes, indiscreetly pointing at figures of interest, and the staff of the theatre seemed on edge. Lazarus had recognized several secret service men in the foyer and at the exits including, bizarrely, Mr. Clumps. He had been given a new mask, which made him look quite theatrical, given the surroundings. He had been lurking at one of the stage doors, and nodded to Lazarus when he had made his way towards the theatre from Exeter Street. Large parts of Covent Garden were cordoned off after the recent street battles, which meant Lazarus had had to pick his way through to the theatre via various side streets. It was a miracle that the Lyceum Theatre was still standing.

Lazarus did not speak to Mr. Clumps. He did not want to distract him while the mechanical was on duty. Besides, their work together was over and Lazarus found himself glad that the bureau still had a use for his old comrade, even if it was only as a bodyguard posted at a stage door.

Lazarus had to admit his surprise at Mansfield's performance. It had not dropped an ounce of its quality or its impact. Once again, Hyde took over and not for the first time, Lazarus wondered at his friend's ability to keep the monster restrained by the limelight and revert to sanity on command. It further confirmed that Hyde could only be released by exposure to the perfumed ointment and at all other times he was a dog on a chain, only revealed in passing glimpses whenever Mansfield's performance required it.

After the brief intermission, Lazarus returned to his box, prepared to let Mansfield see the play to its final curtain before going backstage to tell his friend that it must all stop. At a point nearing the end of the play, he became aware of the curtain behind him being opened a little, letting in some light from the lamp in the hallway. Irritated by the intrusion, he was about to turn and give the usher or the lost patron a piece of his mind when a pair of cold, hard hands grasped him around the neck and began to squeeze with terrific force.

Lazarus shoved his feet against the box's railing and pushed backwards, toppling the chair over on top of whomever it was who was trying to kill him. The grip around his neck loosened and Lazarus struggled to his feet. From the lights reflected off the stage below he could easily see the broad, angular face of his Siamese friend from what felt like a lifetime ago.

The months of working undercover and living life on the edge in the dangerous parts of the East End had sharpened Lazarus's reflexes. He was twice the fighter he had been the last time Westcott's assassin had crossed his path. The Siamese's surprise at this was written on his face as he desperately blocked Lazarus's blows. But even so, Lazarus knew he could not beat him unless he used some cunning.

Offsetting his attacker, Lazarus seized the chair and broke it over his skull before dashing behind the curtain to the corridor beyond. He tried the door at the end of the gallery that led backstage and found it unlocked. Nipping down three steps and around a corner, he waited. The door opened, filling the corridor with light, and his enemy joined him backstage.

Lazarus made his way past the carpenter's shop towards the small box room above the wings that led to the flies; those catwalks where the gas-men hovered above the stage, controlling the lights. Fortunately, there was nobody about and Lazarus did his best to remain in the shadows and out of sight of the gas-men, who could be seen through the tangles of ropes and pulleys, like sailors in the masts of a tall ship.

The assassin entered the room and did not see Lazarus. Lazarus seized a rope that led up into the flies and wound his fists around it, leaving an arm's length between them as if it were a garrote. He fully intended to kill this man. He should have known that Westcott would make another attempt on his life once he had returned from his undercover work. It had to end now, or he would keep finding his life threatened by eastern assassins. When this was all over, he would track down Westcott and there would be a reckoning.

The assassin drew close and Lazarus stepped forward, looping the rope around his neck twice, quick as a cobra, and drawing on the ends tight. The man struggled, but no sound escaped his lips as his windpipe was slowly crushed. Down below, Lazarus could hear the thunderous applause as the play reached its end.

The man in his grip hurled this way and that in an effort to shake him. Lazarus found himself dragged forward towards the iron stairs that led up onto the flies. Below them was a long drop to the wings where the costumed cast huddled, ready to go out onstage for their final bow.

They hit the banister and tumbled over it. The rope whickered taut, and Lazarus felt the snapping of his assailant's neck before gravity tore him away to plummet to the wings below.

Chapter Nineteen

In which an attempt is made on the Prussian chancellor's life

There was so much noise coming from the audience that the sound of Lazarus crashing down into the cluster of stagehands and dressers did not reach beyond those who suddenly found themselves flattened by a man tumbling from the flies. Their cries of alarm and protest were drowned out by the continuing applause.

Lazarus scrambled to his feet and apologized absurdly to those he had landed on. Fortunately, they were much too surprised at his abrupt appearance to look up and notice the dead Siamese man dangling from the flies above them. Any attempt at an explanation on his part quickly became unnecessary, as the cast members were returning to the wings. The curtain had been drawn for the last time, and soon the wings were filled with chattering thespians congratulating each other on a magnificent performance on such a prominent evening.

Mansfield spotted Lazarus and beamed at him. "What a wonderful surprise, Lazarus!" he said, embracing him warmly. "So good of you to come and meet me backstage, but how ever did you get past security? It's tight as a drum tonight with those politicians in the audience. But I'm forgetting your connections, of course!"

"Look, Richard, we need to talk..."

"Of course, of course, we'll go out for drinks afterwards. But the PM and that Bismarck fellow are coming backstage to greet us! Me, meeting the PM! Who'd have thought it?"

"Wonderful, Richard, but..."

"Come on!" Mansfield took Lazarus by the arm and led him through the wings to the dressing rooms. But as they entered the corridor, they saw Stoker leading the delegation towards them. Morton was with them, looking bored. The PM seemed equally uninterested, but there was a smile on the Prussian's face. He extended his hand to Mansfield before there was a chance for introductions to be made.

"The great Mr. Mansfield, of course!" said Bismarck in flawless but accented English. "A wonderful performance, sir! Quite uncanny. You are deserving of your reputation."

He rambled on and Lazarus became aware of a familiar smell; a scent rather, an unusual cologne he knew from somewhere. It seemed to be coming from Bismarck, as if sweated out through the man's pores. As soon as he realized this, he made the connection. *Prussian cologne.*

The change came over Mansfield just as Lazarus realized that he was the only man in the world who could stop the assassination now. Mansfield—or rather, Hyde—let out a bestial cry for blood and lunged forward, raising his silver-topped cane to strike Bismarck a violent blow on the skull. Lazarus grabbed his friend's arm and found himself carried by the force of the blow, and bowled into the Prussian.

All was confusion. Morton's secret service agents

knew that an attempt had been made on the life of the Prussian chancellor, but not by whom. They filed into the narrow corridor from what seemed like several exits, and towering above them was Mr. Clumps, barging his colleagues aside to reach the fray. Lazarus was on top of Bismarck and Mansfield was on top of him. They were a pile of squirming limbs, and Hyde was still trying to kill his target. Lazarus warded off the blows with his forearms, and cried out in agony as the hard, lacquered wood cracked down again and again, bruising him to the bone, but he prevented the deadly silver top from ever striking flesh.

Mr. Clumps seized Mansfield and hauled him off Lazarus. Screeching in frustration, the maniac realized that he had failed his mission. He broke from the mechanical's grip and took off down the corridor, bowling a secret service man over in his wake.

"Get Mansfield!" Lazarus bellowed to Mr. Clumps as several agents seized him and held his arms behind him.

Had he given his order to any other agent, there would no doubt have been some hesitation, but Mr. Clumps knew what Mansfield was and what lurked in his fevered mind. He took off after the actor like a greyhound, his size irrelevant due to his powerful leg mechanisms which carried him down the hall in great bounds.

"Longman, what the hell is going on?" Morton bellowed.

Bismarck was on his feet, and two of his aides had their revolvers drawn and were looking for any excuse to open fire on somebody.

"Mansfield's off his rocker," Lazarus told his chief. "I should have reported him earlier, I know, but I didn't dream that he had this in mind."

"You know that man?"

"We're old friends."

The ruffled delegation made its way out into the foyer, which was now filled with armed bodyguards, both English and Prussian. Lazarus was released after Morton had explained to his agents that he was one of them. The stragglers from the audience were being quickly ushered out into the street. As he watched them leave, Lazarus spotted a face he recognized and let out a curse. *Constantine Westcott!*

He didn't imagine that his villainous cousin had anything to do with the attempt on Bismarck's life, and the dangling Siamese assassin in the flies was proof that Westcott was here for another purpose entirely—to ensure that Lazarus met his end once and for all. But Lazarus simply couldn't let him get away this time. Not now that he finally had a chance to bring his cousin to account for the attempts on his life, and put a halt to the rivalry between them. He had no doubt that the house in Bloomsbury had been emptied—Westcott was too careful to remain there—and he might not get another chance to apprehend his murderous cousin.

As he barged his way through the crowd towards the rain-slicked street outside, he heard Morton exclaim, "Where the devil is he off to now?"

The wet night enveloped them—the pursuer and the pursued—as they dodged carriages that thundered down the street, iron rims skidding on wet stone. Westcott had no time to hail a cab and seemed intent on losing Lazarus on foot. It was a futile plan; Lazarus was far nimbler and quicker than his waifish cousin and would soon be upon him.

Westcott must have known this for he headed

North West, into the cordoned off area of Covent Garden that was little more than rubble. Ducking under a barrier, the pale man scurried down a narrow street that was clogged with piles of masonry and shattered bricks. Following him, Lazarus had no idea if they were on Henrietta Street or King Street, so bombed out was the place. Shells of buildings rose up on all sides; fractured battlements against an iron-black sky from which the rain pelted. There was nobody else within several streets of them. They really had entered a realm of ghosts.

The silence made tracking his quarry easier in the blackened streets. Westcott's hurrying feet splashing through puddles echoed off the fronts of the abandoned buildings and told Lazarus where he was. Rounding a corner, he saw his cousin's dark coattails vanish into an open doorway to a crumbling house. He followed him in and saw the trail of raindrops leading across the polished floorboards to where they soaked into the carpeted stairs.

He climbed the stairs gingerly, wanting Westcott to think he was safe for the time being. He did not know if his cousin was armed but brought out his revolver and cocked it just to be sure.

The landing was in a shambles. Junk left in the wake of the house's departed occupants was strewn about, probably gone over by looters after the shelling. The doors to the first floor rooms hung open. Through them Lazarus could see that half of the building had fallen away and the interior gaped open onto the rain-streaked garden of St. Paul's Church below.

Stepping into what had once been a bedroom, Lazarus saw Westcott cowering behind a chest of drawers, its contents strewn across the floor, trampled by muddy boots. A bed hung precariously over the edge, only three of its four legs touching solid floorboards.

"Your assassin is finished, cousin," Lazarus said, holding his gun up in a gesture that suggested he was not going to shoot just yet.

"I have others," came the arrogant reply.

"Well, unless you've paid them in advance," Lazarus said, "you're going to have a problem seeing that they carry out their assignment. Because I have no intention of giving you the chance to speak with them again."

"What are you going to do? Kill me in cold blood? Your own family?"

The rebuke was absurd, and they both knew it. Westcott was a hypocrite if he thought that would be too callous of Lazarus. But Lazarus was not Constantine Westcott. "I haven't decided yet," he said slowly.

"I don't suppose you'd be willing to cut a deal?" Westcott said. "You have the journal. Have you read it?"

"Yes."

"Then you know what is awaiting you in Siam."

"Not necessarily. A few journal scraps from a man who was given wealth by a king of a secret lost kingdom? That's hardly a legal claim on an inheritance."

"We could go there together! We could find out what happened to your father!"

"Sorry, Constantine. I have no need of you. And besides, he was my father, not yours. Whatever wealth he left is nothing to you while I am still alive."

"You're right," said Westcott. He was standing now, framed against the blackness. "I'm sorry, for what it's worth. I never knew you, and so it was easy to think of you as an unwelcome obstacle to be removed. Perhaps if we had been better acquainted, things might have been different."

"Doubtful," said Lazarus. "A murdering bastard is always a murdering bastard at heart."

"As you say," Westcott replied. He lowered his hands slowly and then, with a sudden movement, thrust his right hand beneath the left breast of his coat.

Lazarus recognized the move for what it was a mile off. Before the cold light glinted off the metal of Constantine's gun barrel, Lazarus squeezed the trigger and sent a bullet directly towards his heart.

It thudded into him and his face turned to one of shock, then horror as the force of it knocked him back a pace. His own gun tumbled from his loose grip and landed heavily on the sodden floorboards. He fell backwards and vanished into the black void.

Lazarus rushed towards the edge. It was difficult to differentiate the black shapes below in the garden of St. Paul's Church; there was a bench, and a pile of rubble that had slid away from one of the bombed buildings, there a dresser, upended, and there... there was Constantine Westcott's body, smashed and motionless, his coat tails spread out around him like the wings of a fallen angel.

When Lazarus arrived back at the Lyceum, he found several police officers milling about. There was no sign of Morton or any of the delegation, and so he introduced himself to the inspector who was conducting the investigation.

"You'd best get over to Leman Street," said the inspector. "Use my cab."

"They're in Whitechapel? Why?"

"There's been developments. The would-be assassin has been killed. Apparently he was come upon while trying to get into a place on Miller's Court. Probably seeking refuge with an acquaintance."

The news that Mansfield was dead was only surpassed in Lazarus's mind by the words 'Miller's Court'. That could only mean Mary. What in God's name had happened?

He found Leman Street nearly bursting with coppers and secret service men. Wading through to the sergeant's desk, he saw Morton through the glass of Inspector Read's office door, talking to Mary. He barged in, wanting to scoop the girl up in an embrace, but stopped himself within a few feet of her.

"Ah, you're alive," he said, lamely. "Jolly good."

Her face did not have any of the crackling energy it usually burned with. She seemed thoroughly down, as if all the joy had been sucked out of her.

Morton broke in before she had a chance to speak. "Longman, I haven't the faintest idea where you charged off to earlier but we shall get to the bottom of that in due course. Right now we have bigger fish to fry. I'm afraid your friend is dead."

"So I heard," Lazarus said. "But what the devil happened? I sent Mr. Clumps after him. What was he doing at Miss Kelly's place?"

"That was an order you had no right to give," said Morton, his voice stern. "You are on leave of absence and were at the theatre as a civilian. Any orders given to my men should have come from me."

"Come off it, Morton," said Lazarus. "Are you really going to come down on me like that for doing exactly what you would have done? Mansfield, friend of mine though he was, tried to kill Bismarck. He needed to be caught!"

"And caught he may have been had somebody else been sent. Mr. Clumps is an experimental measure and cannot be trusted with delicate orders. Surely I don't have to remind you of this."

"Are you telling me that..."

"Clumps killed Mansfield, yes. With his bare hands. Practically tore him apart like a wild animal."

"I need to speak to him."

"I think we should stop referring to it as a person," Morton said. "It is a machine, after all, for all its human characteristics."

"What's going to happen to him?" Lazarus asked.

"Decommissioned. We can't trust a thing like that wandering around. Not with that kind of strength. We're not Americans yet."

"Decommissioned? You mean executed?"

"Call it what you like. Its service to us is at an end."

Mr. Clumps was being held in one of the cells. He sat, patiently, his massive forearms resting on those boulders that served as knees, and his head low. The cell was damp with his steam, condensed on the rough walls, and made the atmosphere heavily oppressive.

"Why did you do it, man?" Lazarus asked, once he had convinced the copper on guard to leave him alone with the murderer. "Couldn't you have brought him in alive? Was he really so violent that you had to..."

"After what he tried to do, yes," came the reply. "I would have killed him a hundred times over if I could. I didn't know the other girls but when I think of Mary and what his intentions were I get... *confused*."

"He tried to kill Mary?"

"Yes, I followed him all the way to Whitechapel. Why was he there? Why Mary? I don't understand!"

The mechanical's voice seemed to be injected with some emotion which Lazarus found heartbreaking to hear. He remembered how Mr. Clumps and Mary had eventually taken to each other, like a big gentle bear playing with a little girl. It seemed that he had developed some sort of feelings for her, simple things such as they were. *A mechanical with a heart...*

"Hyde wanted to kill her," Lazarus told him. "After failing to kill the Prussian, he took off, hoping to fulfill his bloodlust elsewhere. Like when he killed Catherine Eddowes after I interrupted his mutilation of Elizabeth Stride. Once that monster is set in motion only blood can pacify him."

"But why Mary? He would have encountered plenty of prostitutes between the Lyceum and Miller's Court."

"Because of me," said Lazarus. "He wanted to kill her to hurt me."

"I'm sorry, Lazarus. I couldn't help myself. I knew it was wrong and yet I could not stay my hands."

"Don't apologize," Lazarus said. "You did perhaps what I had not the courage to do."

"They'll put me out of use now, won't they? Take me apart."

"I'll put in a good word," Lazarus said. "See what I can do..." He was a liar and he knew it. He wouldn't be able to convince them. He was the only person in the world who understood what had happened. How could anybody else even begin to comprehend a mechanical's devotion to a common whore? Mr. Clumps would take the fall. The murders in Whitechapel would stop and the Ripper's identity would never be known. And Lazarus would say nothing. He owed Mansfield that courtesy. His memory must not be tarnished for the sake of the good man who had fought and lost the battle against his dark half. The working girls of Whitechapel were safe, or at least a little safer. That was what was important.

Mr. Clumps jetted out a cloud of steam and lowered his cigar. "I failed my makers," he said. "I'm supposed to protect lives, not take them. I'm supposed to mirror the compassion of human beings. But I killed a man. It's because I'm too much a machine, isn't it?"

"No," Lazarus replied. "It's because you're too much a man."

Chapter Twenty

In which Lime Kiln Dock receives its final sacrifice

Mary was gone from the inspector's office when Lazarus returned. He found Morton reading a note from the telegraph operator. "God, what a night!" Morton said.

"What's up now?" Lazarus asked him.

"I've had our fellows keeping their eyes open for Pedachenko these last few days," Morton said.

"And now he's been spotted? Tonight?"

Morton nodded. "In Limehouse. Our agent lost visual contact, but he's there somewhere. We need to get all our lot over there right now and close the net before he stows away on some steamer. Can I count on you too?"

"Of course," Lazarus said, but he was already on his way out of the office.

Limehouse. There was just one final piece of the puzzle that eluded him, and he was confident he knew where he would find the answer.

The old lime oast he had visited twice before began to feel like an old, down-and-out but familiar friend. There was nobody about as Lazarus stepped down from the cab and headed towards the entrance.

There was evidence of some activity in the dusty interior. Boxes, open and empty, lay discarded on the dockside, almost unnoticed by Lazarus as he gazed with widening eyes on the extraordinary sight before him. In that one glimpse of the fantastical, all of his questions were answered. He now knew why Mansfield had been depositing his grisly trophies into the grim water of the Limehouse Basin. They were not sacrifices, but signs; breadcrumbs left in the woods for him to follow.

Mansfield had known what was concealed beneath those waters. Even with Hyde running rampant in his fevered brain, driving his movements, he had still managed to do these final, desperate acts after each murder while his mind writhed with revulsion at his own actions.

It was not a huge thing; no bigger than its cousins Lazarus had seen in America. Its shiny surface glistened with the moisture and green slime hung in great clumps from it; evidence that it had been submerged for quite some time. Made of greenish copper, it was inlaid with brass hatches and a bulbous glass dome formed its front, resembling a huge, hideous eye. And within that eye, like dark thoughts seen through the window to the soul, Lazarus could see movement.

This was a contraption for one or two men at most, designed for infiltration rather than warfare; the perfect vehicle for sneaking along London's waterways. This was how Pedachenko intended to escape to Russia. It would not take him all the way, of course, being a short distance vehicle, but Lazarus did not doubt that a larger vessel would meet it somewhere in the North Sea to carry it home.

Sounds came from within its iron hull as the crew prepared for voyage. Lazarus wasted no time and made a flying leap onto its slimy sides. Scrabbling for grip, he managed to grasp the open hatch cover and pull himself on top. He peered down and saw no sign of anybody directly below him. Drawing his revolver, he clambered down the iron rungs and boarded the craft.

A world of brass dials, enamel levers and glass-covered valves greeted him, all lit by the flickering of a nearby gas lamp. The craft was long and tubular in design, intersected by wheel lock doors. Up ahead, he could see the cockpit with the pilot making ready. Lazarus wondered that the skipper had not gone mad all alone in this metal cigar at the bottom of Limehouse Basin for God knows how long. Trips to the surface for air and supplies must have been strictly limited for the sake of security.

It seemed too easy. Kill the skipper and Pedachenko wasn't going anywhere. There was a noise behind him and Lazarus scrambled behind some sort of machinery that led from the boiler to the screw, just in time to avoid being seen by the Pedachenko himself as he emerged from the aft, having deposited some cargo. He stopped to secure the hatch Lazarus had just passed through, sealing the three of them in together.

Calling out something in Russian to the skipper, Pedachenko walked right by Lazarus, ignorant of the intruder. The boiler had already been ticking over, and the skipper engaged some mechanism that began the turning of the screw. Lazarus became aware of movement as the submarine drifted gently forward. It also began, alarmingly, to sink. If he was going to act before they got out on the open sea, then he had better do it as soon as possible.

He rose, revolver in hand, and advanced on the cockpit. He could see the skipper's back, hunched over the controls, but of Pedachenko there was no sign. A shot rang out, deafening in the close quarters, the flash of gunpowder lighting up the cockpit. The bullet missed Lazarus but hit something behind him, sending off sparks.

Lazarus replied with two shots of his own. At least one hit the skipper in the back, sending him lurching forward, blood spattering the glass dials.

"It's over!" Lazarus called out to Pedachenko. "This craft will never leave the Thames."

"Mr. Longman," came the Russian drawl. "Your ability to survive does not cease to amaze me. I had you down as dead in the rubble of London, as so many are."

"Thanks to you."

"I was merely a figurehead. I'm not the megalomaniacal puppet master you may see me as. The people of London were revolutionists without a banner long before I came to this city. All they needed was a push in the right direction. I'm rather proud of them, aren't you? Who would have thought that the great British Empire was nearly overturned by a rabble of tailors, machinists and dockers?"

"Those people were free and innocent before you meddled with their brains and turned them into monsters."

"How naive you are. I merely had to fine-tune them, and only a handful at that. The rest were just begging for somebody to believe in, somebody other than your government and your queen. If I had not fitted the glass slipper, then no doubt somebody else would have done so in one year, five or ten. Your empire is doomed, you see? Your own people can't even stand to be its subjects."

"Aren't you denying yourself some credit?" Lazarus asked. "You fine-tuned a handful perhaps, but what tuning! You would give the zombi-makers of Haiti a run for their money in manipulating people to do your will, like mannequins dancing on fishing line. One of them was my friend and that is why I am going to kill you."

"Your friend? I must say, you have me at a disadvantage."

"Richard Mansfield. Learn the name, because I want it to be on your mind when your life leaves your body."

"You can't bring down an empire without breaking a few minds," said Pedachenko with a daring smile. "I'm sorry if I upset you, but a government agent like yourself must understand the necessities of war."

"Necessities of war," said Lazarus. "Pawns, you mean. To be sacrificed like sheep to some god who will never reveal himself? And let's not forget the side effects of your manipulations. In your eagerness to fulfill your mission, you have been responsible for the most diabolical series of murders this country has ever known."

"You mean the whores of Whitechapel? How were we to know that Mansfield was a maniac? Those victims are his and his alone. And the lunatic even kept bringing their body parts back here to pelt at this submarine like some sort of shit-chucking chimp."

Lazarus found himself capable of a short laugh. "You bastards made a monster that you were unable to control. And his madness brought me right to you."

"Yes, very handy. A final loose end for me to tie up."

A deadly hail of bullets went Lazarus's way and he

rolled to the left, miraculously dodging the rain of death. The sound of them ricocheting off metallic surfaces could be heard at the bottom of the hallway, as well as the smashing of glass as several instruments were destroyed.

Lazarus opened fire but found himself shooting at empty air, for Pedachenko had vanished back into the cockpit. His bullets thudded through the glass canopy and water began leaking in, like fountains spat from the mouths of cherubs.

Lazarus dodged another two bullets as he got to his feet, but then heard the Russian's gun clicking empty. He cast his own aside. He wanted to kill Pedachenko with his bare hands and he knew he was capable of it.

As he entered the cockpit, his adversary gave up reloading his revolver and hurled himself at him. They hit the deck together and rolled, each trying to lock his hands around the other's throat. Lazarus wound up on top, letting Pedachenko do his damndest to strangle him while he contented himself with pounding the Russian's face with both fists.

Blood leaked away from mouth and nostrils to mix with the muddy Thames water that sloshed around them. Pedachenko spluttered as he got a mouthful and Lazarus grabbed his throat and squeezed, letting his bodyweight do most of the work. His thumbs dug into the Russian's windpipe and the rising water aided him in his butchery. Pedachenko's face was submerged. He mouthed vain pleas beneath a murky, swirling vortex.

When the body beneath him went slack, Lazarus released his fingers and realized that he had been screaming the whole time. He stood up. The water was up to his knees. Pedachenko was lost beneath the lapping tide that was filling the cockpit and rushing down the length of the submarine.

There was a shuddering jolt that nearly knocked Lazarus off his swaying feet as the vessel hit the bottom of Limehouse Basin. Only then did he remember that he was locked in a metal tube many feet underwater.

He waded his way towards the hatch, and as he clambered up the ladder he knew it was useless to try and open it. He tried anyway, and it wouldn't budge. The hatch would never open until the pressure within the submarine matched the pressure without. And that left plenty of time for drowning.

It was an agonizing wait as the water level rose, inch by inch. Lazarus wished he had shot more holes through the cockpit canopy just to speed up the inevitable. He clung to the ladder as the water rose up around his chest. Soon his head was bobbing against the hatch like a cork that had been pushed too far down into a bottle. He took a deep breath as it reached his chin and began to fill his ears.

When he was completely submerged he tried the hatch again. It still would not budge. He didn't know how long he could hold out if the equalizing of pressure took much longer. His lungs began to scream for air and he scrabbled at the wheel lock again. It gave a little, but the outside pressure was still very strong. Jamming his feet against the rungs of the ladder, he heaved with all his might. The lid cracked open a little, then a little further, getting easier with every inch he forced it.

Finally, it swung open and clanged back against the hull. Lazarus shot from the opening like a launched torpedo. Kicking for all he was worth, he wound his way to the surface and broke through it with a gasp of freedom.

"Our teams are dredging Limehouse Basin as we speak," said Morton, handing Lazarus a brandy. "They'll turn up Pedachenko's corpse sooner or later. And that submarine too. That will be the real treasure. It sounds fabulously advanced and we can only guess at how its capture will affect our own naval developments. And you're sure it was not powered by mechanite?"

"Certain," said Lazarus sipping at his brandy. He was in dry clothes and the fire in Morton's office crackled merrily, but he still felt cold and damp. "Why would you think that the Russians would have any mechanite?"

"Troubling reports from Alaska," said Morton.

"Alaska?" Lazarus said. That's still Russian territory, isn't it?"

"Yes, and dangerously close to the United States. The concerns of two decades ago that the Russians might sell the colony to the U.S. out of fear that we would take it from them in war came to nothing. But their reasons for holding on to it may present an even greater problem. The Tsar's support of the U.S. is a badly-kept secret, but he has been prevented from openly giving aid to them by the fear of war with us. Now it seems his courage has been bolstered."

"How so?"

"Factories springing up in the easternmost parts of Siberia. Nothing to do with the fur trade. These are war factories, right on the United States' doorstep."

"Are they planning to take British Colombia? That

would mean all-out war with us."

"Certainly, but we fear that their intentions are even worse than that. Infrastructure seems to have increased on both sides of the Bering Strait. There has long been an idea that the strait could be crossed by three bridges via the two Diomede Islands. Such a plan has been proven troublesome due to weather conditions. But our sources say that it is not impossible for some sort of tunneling program to succeed where an overland crossing might fail. You yourself have witnessed the effectiveness of steam-driven tunneling machines."

"Yes, beneath the deserts of Arizona. But what use would it be to join Alaska with Siberia?"

"If a formal alliance exists between Russia and the United States, then such a tunnel from Cape Prince of Wales to Cape Vostochny would be an immense advantage to them. Men and supplies could be ferried between continents in less than a day. And we fear that the U.S. may even renege on the mechanite embargo which, until now, both the U.S. and the C.S. have abided by. Russia's eternal support could be bought with just a few tons of the stuff."

"Meaning bad news for us," said Lazarus thoughtfully. "And if the U.S. dealt mechanite to the Russians, perhaps the Confederates would be willing to trade with us, which is, I imagine, the very thing you fellows are hoping for."

"You're not wrong, Lazarus."

"Christ, it could mean a world war!"

"Yes, and we need to make sure we are ahead of the game before it starts. I have spoken with the PM and we have been drawing up plans for espionage missions in Siberia. The Russians have already tried to strike us a death blow with Pedachenko's faux revolution, but their failure will only spur them on in their wish to see us defeated. I'm glad you're back on board, Longman. The near future could prove extremely exciting."

The customers of the *Ten Bells* showed no signs of having just emerged from a bloody revolution. 'Life goes on' seemed to be the words on everybody's lips as Lazarus walked up to the crowded bar and ordered a pint of porter. He wished those words might come easier to him.

He saw Mary up ahead, entertaining a couple of sailors in a booth with a friend. One of them would be her first customer of the night, and Lazarus had no intention of interfering. He would come back another night to say what he had to say to her.

Then again, maybe not.

He wanted to tell her that they would not be seeing each other again. His continuing work with the government was too consuming, not to mention dangerous for everybody in his life. That was why the bureau preferred its agents to remain unmarried; no luggage or private entanglements to complicate things. After all, look what had nearly happened to her just because she had met him a few short weeks ago.

No, he could not protect her, and to pretend that he could was a dangerous kind of arrogance. He had failed in his promises to her; she had nearly become Jack the Ripper's final victim. And the thought of yet another woman dead because of him was not something he could bear. She could make her own way in the world, he was sure of that, and any kind of relationship with him would only end in disaster.

He would always wonder if it could have worked between them; a government agent and an east end prostitute. He imagined them living in a pleasant house outside of London or perhaps in the West Country, free from all the troubles of their pasts. But he knew it was a mere pipedream; something comforting to chew over on lonely nights when he was far from home on government business.

Besides, there was another woman out there who had taken his heart and had still not given it back.

He left his pint unfinished and headed for the door. Mary had not noticed him and he wanted to keep it that way. It was better that they remained figures from the past for each other. He exited the pub and jammed his bowler hat on, thrusting his hands deep into his pockets as he walked away, letting the onyx shadows of the city swallow him.

Epilogue

The cold wind blasting down the tunnel ahead of the locomotive was almost as cold as it would have been up on the surface. Katarina Mikolavna hunched her shoulders in an attempt to block the chill seeping down the sheepskin collar of her jacket.

Being underground was only slightly better than being topside. These Russian industrial complexes and military installations were cold places at the best of times; harsh, grey and utilitarian. But at least she was out of the fierce Siberian winds that whipped across the frozen Bering Strait to scour the bleak headlands. Those winds felt like they could strip the flesh from your face.

The train thundered out of the black tunnel in a cloud of vapor, its brakes screeching as it drew to a halt. It was a massive thing, all blackened iron and steaming pistons. The cranes dangled overhead, ready to pick up the materials from the oblong goods carriages below. Workers scurried along the walkways overhead like ants in a colony.

The door to the guard van opened and the colonel stepped down, his fur-trimmed cloak reaching below the tops of his black lacquered boots. Katarina felt her heart hammering in her chest as he approached, just as it had always done when she had been a little girl and he had returned from one of his journeys to

Petersburg. The colonel was a big man and had a habit of making every room, no matter how huge, seem barely adequate to contain him. Katarina always thought that he would make the interior of Saint Isaac's Cathedral seem like a peasant's cottage if he stood beneath its dome.

"Any news on our agent's progress in London?" he demanded of her without any greeting.

"Reports say that he struck earlier than planned and nearly brought the city to its knees."

"Nearly?"

"We could hardly have expected him to have brought the British Empire down singlehandedly, Colonel. His provocations were, after all, merely a diversion."

"A diversion that was spent too early and thus rendered useless to us. What are his reasons for this premature strike?"

"That's a bit of a mystery. He has not yet returned to us, and so we have been unable to put together a satisfying report."

"And Bismarck is dead?"

"Ah... no," Katarina said, hating the way her taut nerves made her voice waver as if she were afraid. "That's also a bit of a mystery. It seems Pedachenko's plan was foiled."

The colonel sucked the chill air into his lungs, as if sieving it through his moustache, catching invisible particles like a baleen whale. "Foiled." The word was not a question. "I always said the Interior Ministry put too much faith in his hocus pocus. All that babble about mind control. The man belonged in a fairground. And maybe that's where he'll end up if he ever dares to return to us. I suppose his subject decided to eat his own shoes or something instead of killing Bismarck?"

"Actually it looks as if Pedachenko's work on his subject was successful but the assassination was interrupted at the last minute by somebody, perhaps by accident. We don't know."

"A washout all round, then. The failures of other agents only increase the burden on us. We must pick up the slack or all is lost. Have you visited the factories?"

"Yes. It's all most... impressive."

"Merely impressive? You always were one who lacked imagination, girl. This is the future of the Russian Empire, born right here on Cape Vostochny. This latest shipment of mechanite will speed up our experiments vastly."

"How long until they will be ready for use in the field?"

"Difficult to say. Holdups are due to, as always, human error. The mechanical part is flawless. Less flawless are the pilots' dexterity in wielding them. But with sufficient training they will overcome all obstacles."

They had left the station now and were making their way into the cavernous hanger where a variety of vehicles were docked. Sparks flew from the welder's torch and lit up the place in eclectic bursts. The doors at the far end were open and snow blown on the chill blast whirled in.

A transportation vehicle was waiting for them, its mechanite furnace keeping a head of steam ready. A hatch in the side opened onto a warm interior with two double seats in black leather facing each other.

Once they were seated, the driver slammed the hatch shut and clambered into his own seat on top, which was enclosed within a dome-like turret that would protect him from the elements. It was stiflingly hot within, and Katarina had to loosen her fur-lined jacket. The colonel did not move, being a man indifferent to changes in temperature.

The vehicle's tracks grated and it rumbled off. Through the thick glass in the narrow window slits, Katarina could see the walls of the hanger quickly replaced by the frozen Siberian landscape beneath the black night.

"I expect a report on your progress in identifying the leak in our operations once we are finished touring the factories," the colonel told her.

"Colonel," Katarina began, having dreaded this part of her superior's return most of all, "there has been very little progress, I must be honest with you."

"I see."

"Whoever is leaking the information to the revolutionaries must be contacting someone in one of the villages. And these villages are so few and far between that it is impossible for me to be in all places at once. By the time I have reached one trading post, they have long since moved on."

"I would have expected you to have recruited local help in your task."

"I have tried but the people in these parts, few as they are, are not sympathetic to the Tsar's agents. I have even tried the Yupik people but they are even less inclined to help."

"They are savages," the colonel replied. "You won't get anything from them unless you speak to them in their own language; savagery. You still have your armed units?"

"Yes, but are you suggesting that I tear apart native

settlements looking for revolutionaries? They are not known to mix."

"I am suggesting that you do your job, agent! Need I remind you that your continued career with the Interior Ministry is due only to the fact that I am your uncle?"

Katarina felt her cheeks burning as she stared at the floor of the vehicle. She needed no reminding. After the confusing series of events in the C.S.A. that still had the ministry baffled, and her failure to procure Dr. Lindholm in Egypt, her career should have been over. Two failures were two more than were usually tolerated.

"I brought you here to act under my supervision in a rare moment of sentimentality," the colonel went on. "I require you to root out this traitor while I oversee the security of our operations in our colony across the strait. A third failure on your part will not only end your career but will humiliate me. And that is something neither of us can afford."

"Yes, uncle," Katarina replied in a small voice, suddenly feeling ten years old again.

They rumbled into the factory complex and the iron doors wheeled shut behind them. Katarina was sweltering in her furs but knew better than to undo her jacket. As soon as they stepped out of the vehicle, the icy hanger instantly reminded her that she was at the very edge of the world, beyond sunlight and warmth.

In the chamber beyond stood the finished products of Russia's top secret program; Project Ironman. They were lined up three ranks deep like terracotta warriors, awaiting the spell that would bring them to life. But it was no magic rites that would power these machine men. Each of them had a seat within their iron exteriors where one of the Tsar's finest would sit, warmed by the mechanite furnace beneath him and the boiler carried on its back. Legs and arms would be strapped in, encased in armor and vision of the battlefield would be provided by the slit of darkened glass in the bucket-shaped helmet.

"A massive improvement on those monstrosities they use in the Americas," the Colonel said. "Sometimes simpler is better. No need for mind control or barbaric surgery. These things can be driven like tanks. And our pilots are so much more trustworthy than the brainwashed half-men people like Pedachenko want us to use."

Katarina barely heard her uncle. As she gazed over the arrayed ranks of super soldiers she felt more lost than ever. The world was going to hell and her country was carrying the battle standard.

Her feelings confused her. At the beginning of her career she might have wished to pilot one of these terrifying machines herself, to lead her country to greatness. But these days she felt different somehow. Changed. She wasn't sure how it had come about. All she knew was that she blamed one man in particular; a man she had been unable to forget since she had left him in Paris two years ago.

As they passed the ranks of mechanized suits of armor, she glanced briefly at the white stenciling on their sides. Each showed the make and serial number along with a single word; the Russian word for 'ironman'. It said

Ле́нин

(Lenin)

A Note from the Author

I hope you have enjoyed *Onyx City,* the third novel in the Lazarus Longman Chronicles. You could be very kind and leave a review on Amazon or your retailer of choice, or even just recommend it to somebody. Check out my blog at www.pjthorndyke.wordpress.com where I post about all things Steampunk.

I'm also active on;
Facebook (@PJThorndykeAuthor),
Instagram (pjthorndyke_author)
and Twitter (@PJThorndyke).

Look out for future adventures of Lazarus Longman!

Printed in Great Britain
by Amazon

64916461R00149